THE PALE SERGEANT

THE PALE SERGEANT

James Murray

Chatto & Windus

LONDON

With the exception of pale Sergeant Death,
the characters in this book are entirely imaginary
and bear no relation to any living person.

Published in 1986 by
Chatto & Windus Ltd
40 William IV Street
London WC2N 4DF

ISBN 0-7011-3960-9

Printed and bound in Great Britain by
Butler & Tanner Ltd, Frome and London

TO
MY WIFE, JENNY,
WITHOUT WHOM . . .

'When pale Sergeant Death shall in his arms enfold me ...'
Scottish song

'Had I but time, as this fell sergeant, death,
Is strict in his arrest, O, I could tell you –
But let it be ...'
Hamlet, Act 5, Scene 2

I

The coffin floated on the crest of a wave, a wave of sand, outrider
to an ocean of sand, the dried blood of Australia's dead heart,
rolling from the west to be checked by a line of gum trees growing
along the river which snaked from a rocky gorge to the north.

On the lid of the coffin was a scrawled square of cardboard,
weighted with a can of beer. Under the lid of the coffin, Ogilvie,
A., Trooper, 621, lay dreaming.

Wind from the crack of dawn clicked in a nearby windmill,
becoming in Ogilvie's dream the rifle bolt rattle of a firing squad
aiming at him.

'Easy!' Ogilvie shouted in his dream. 'Easy! Sergeant Death!'

The firing squad did not shoot, but began the slow drill of
reversing arms, their hands on the rifles becoming skeletal.

The wind still clicked in the windmill so that the sun rose as if
it were being jacked up. Its first rays struck the can of beer on the
coffin lid. The can twinkled blue and gold and the coffin lid turned
from black to shiny, varnished cedar. The ocean of sand turned red
and east of the river a great plain whispered where the wind was
caught by tussocks of grey-green, spiky grass.

The chill of the night passed with the first fly hum. A mob of
goats bleated, tittupping from their night paddock, near the one-
pub town of Rainbow, to forage on the plain.

The mongrel Dustbin, like a patch left over from the night,
watched the goats foraging. Here, a clump of pigweed. There, a
cigarette packet. All the time, the goats moved closer to the river
by which Dustbin lay in wait. Her dingo mate, as quietly as a ginger
cloud, trotted towards the goats from a clump of grey scrub. The
goats milled in panic. Dustbin struck from their flank, snarling.
She downed a kid in a drench of blood, dragging it into a gully

where her dingo mate joined her silently to rip the throat from the kid.

The mob of goats, led by a billy wearing a clanking neck bell, fled across the river towards the coffin. They halted as from the coffin came the sound of a man gasping in an extremity of regret, gasping, 'Shug, Shug, I'm right sorry for what I did to you,' gasping, 'God, I thought I had time.'

The billy goat wheeled, its neck bell clanking more loudly, as it led the mob from the coffin.

Ogilvie, half out, half in his dream of death, rose up for judgement, sending the coffin lid thudding on the sand, the cardboard flying and the can of beer rolling.

He looked towards the rising sun and rubbed his face with his hands, washing himself with the light of the new day he hadn't expected to see.

'The so-and-sos,' he shouted, staring down into the coffin, its white padding marked by the cold sweat of his dream. 'The cheeky so-and-sos.'

He stepped from the coffin, dressed in a torn blue shirt, khaki shorts and a pair of old, black Army-issue boots. 'Get away with you,' he shouted to the goats. 'Get away.'

The billy goat gave him a wall-eyed stare and ducked its horns at him. He rubbed his own eyes. 'Maybe, you're right. Maybe, it's me that's the goat.'

He went to the square of cardboard annd read the scrawl on it:

Og
Drink in Peace
Down
Under

Vin and the boys, of course. But Vin's writing. And Vin's joke. He gave himself away all the time.

8

Ogilvie picked up the cardboard and skimmed it high into the sun. He went down to where the can of beer lay, ripped it open and drank and spat in disgust and prayed again, 'Oh God, don't send me to hell if it means warm Aussie beer.'

The can rose from his hand, trailing beer. It landed among the mob of goats, scattering them as if it were a tear-gas canister and they were people.

Ogilvie ran from those memories, ran towards the line of gum trees – a procession with banners; ran fast, dodging among termite towers – lads standing with stones in their hands; ran towards the rocky gorge and the river – a city divided by bloodshed; ran, forcing his booze-heavy legs to go faster, faster as his breath came in heaving gasps which echoed the names sounding in his memory – Rodd. McAskill. Belfast. Ireland.

2

The mob of goats moved towards a huddle of humpies, patched together from timber, flattened oil drums, rusty corrugated-iron sheets, canvas bags and cardboard. One nanny goat turned off the track to chew a piece of cardboard flapping from the side of the biggest humpy. The billy wearing the neck bell ranged ahead of the mob to sniff at the sand-shredded tyres of an old car. His neck bell clanked.

Inside the old car, Vin Sheean stirred in his sleep. His white hand rose up, clenching, to be caught by the black hand of Bel Maley. He opened his mouth to speak. She laid her hand on his mouth.

'No more,' she said. 'Beating your chest allersame Tarzan and all that monkey yabber.'

9

Awakening, Sheean grinned. 'Who's the driver of this limousine?'

She led his hand to where she wanted to bring him again. 'You. You been there all night like old man. Kiss me properly.'

'Me? Break the first bush commandment and smooch with a gin? You've got to be joking.'

His smiling mouth went to hers. His hand moved up to her breast as she turned to find him again. The plank bed, jammed above the dashboard and the back window ledge, groaned.

'The festive board,' said Sheean.

'Poem,' said Bel.

'Have to be dactylic.' Sheean began to tickle her and she giggled as he said 'The Marquis of Montrose to His Mistress' and recited, still tickling:

> ' "My dear and only love, I pray
> This noble world of thee,
> Be governed by no other sway,
> But purest Monarchie . . ." '

Bel shrieked with laughter. 'Not that one. Other.'

Sheean kissed her and said, 'Maybe you should get Og to recite it for you. It's really his recitation.'

'That Og mighty man,' said Bel.

'Yeah, but you should hear him say that poem when he's shickered. Get laughs from a heart of stone. Last night, he got so shickered we –'

'Know that,' said Bel. 'Other poem. Your poem. No tickling.'

'Shut up,' said Sheean and went on, 'How beautiful art thou, my love, how beautiful are thou. Thy eyes are dove's eyes beside what is hid within. Thy hair is as a flock of goats which come from mount Galaad. Thy teeth –'

Bel giggled as the billy's bell clanked again.

'Can't you be serious?' said Sheean. But he knew she could. She had been serious in the night, wanting, wanting a child from him, though she still only half believed what they did together made a child, preferring the immemorial belief of her people, the kuri people, that what they did together simply summoned the spirit of a child waiting. She was serious again now, trying to hold him, panting, 'Don't. Don't,' as he pulled himself out of her to spill his seed on the straw palliasse covering the plank bed.

'Plurry wanker,' Bel said.

And Sheean wondered what Onan's woman had said to Onan, the original poor, bloody wanker from Genesis, chapter thirty-eight, verse nine.

Sheean sought Bel's breast. Easier stifling conscience than memory.

3

Halliday patted the bulging breast pockets of his safari jacket as he stared out at the starboard prop of his chartered aircraft catching the sun light and spinning it into a golden halo. Heading north in Australia, he thought. Outback bound. Or Further In, as he'd heard guys say who actually seemed to have got beyond the last suburban rancho with the plaster *peon* in the patio.

Halliday unfastened his seat belt and stood up. He was slightly stooped in the way of massive men used to avoiding bumping their heads in doorways. He patted the side pockets of his safari jacket and the breast pockets again.

Then he leaned down and patted Sue Cornwall as familiarly as he had patted his own breast pockets. 'Got a cigar for your old man, Bibi?'

She shifted in her seat. 'I'm not your cigar case. Stop pawing me.'

'Come on now, Bibi. You can't expect to get your own way all the time.'

'I didn't bargain for this.'

'But you did bargain.'

'Not for this.'

'It'll be good for you, Bibi. Outback. The Bush.'

'Don't call me Bibi.'

'Educational. Like Bibi means young maiden in Swahili. You objecting to the adjective or the noun?'

'I'm objecting to being shanghaied on a mad trip to nowhere.'

'Now, Bibi. That's not the way to speak of your own country. You told me you wanted to see it again. Told me in London. Remember?' He touched her auburn hair. 'Beautiful. Truly. The French call your kind of hair *blond ardent*. Burning fair. Glowing fair. Passionate fair.'

She pulled her head away from his stroking. 'What's the French for "Naff off"?' she said. And after a pause, 'Tembo.'

'Passionate is right. You Bibi, maiden. Me Tembo, elephant.'

She had been staring out of the window, imagining that the clouds were castles. She turned to look at him and he saw his age in her young green eyes. 'I'm sick of you.' Again the pause. 'Tembo. Your instant analysis of everyone except yourself. I mean, what are we doing? I was under the impression you had enough material about Oz, and that we were catching a scheduled flight back to London. Then New York.'

'Change of plans. I want to see the Bush.'

'Not enough applause in the cities, I suppose.'

'Missed by a mile, Bibi.' He ran his fingers through his white hair, grimacing as if he'd just drunk a slug of bad whisky. Yeah, she had missed all right. By a mile. And a metastasis. She'd been gossiping with Ashby, of course. Lewis Ashby, aka Fisi, the entrail-eating hyena. He didn't know either. Fisi didn't know.

Wouldn't he have loved to have been sniffing around, clicking and whirring, goddamn robot hyena, Fisi, with his motorised camera eye, when that vulture-headed witch doctor in Sydney had flapped his black X-ray-plate wings and squawked the verdict.

Sue Cornwall said, 'It's not too late to go back.'

Halliday peered down at a river, edged with green, curving and looping back on itself. Without looking at Sue Cornwall, he patted her knee. 'It is for me, Bibi. Point of no return. So you might as well get changed. Rough country ahead. No castles. Glass slippers no good.'

She stared at him. He seemed to be able to get into her mind. He knew she'd been imagining the clouds were castles. She stood up, pulled a tote bag from the seat in front and began stripping off the silk red-and-blue patchwork dressing gown she'd kept on as a protest against being rousted out early on a Sunday for a flight she didn't want.

The pilot, Tucker, his snaggleteeth and boyish face making his microphone and earphones like some kind of elaborate dental brace, looked over his shoulder. Seeing the woman so tall, and as naked as the sky, with the red-gold cloud between her legs no bigger than a man's hand, he let out a yell and put the aircraft into a banking turn. Sue Cornwall fell towards Halliday who caught her, kissed her and would've held her except that the aircraft was in level flight again so that she was able to pull away from him.

'You told me to change,' she said.

Halliday grinned. 'That mouth of yours, Bibi. It's never going to be puritan. Rough country ahead, sure. Big, too. But plenty of – ' Halliday mock stuttered – 'F-f-f-flying time.'

She ignored him. He watched her dressing. The same casual, model's speed with which she'd undressed: black panties, what he called burnt bra – none, blue jeans, big, white cotton shirt. A black belt decorated with ammunition loops and soft, black leather boots

13

into which she tucked her jeans. He must be getting old. Dress tease more interesting than strip tease.

He helped himself to a whisky from the liquor cabinet. Yeah, definitely getting old. Second adolescence. Second childhood coming up fast. And after that, second birth, aka death.

Fisi might not know about the witch doctor's verdict. He'd sure as hell sensed second birth coming. Which was why Fisi'd put together a joint project. Australia A–Z. Words Scott Halliday. Pictures Lewis Ashby.

Yeah, and coming soon. The Long, Killing Life of Scott Halliday. Words and pictures, Lewis Ashby.

Maybe he should make Fisi a present of Long, Killing Life title. Halliday patted the side pocket of his safari jacket. The hell with it, Fisi was a scavenger. He could scavenge for his own title. Tembo Halliday and I. Something like that.

4

Ogilvie jumped from the edge of the gorge into the river. Just before he hit the water, rising like milky tea to meet him, he felt the memory jerk of parachute harness. As the jump took him under, the water changed to green. The pounding of blood in his ears was the beating of drums in Belfast with pig-snouted, goggled-eyed squaddies doubling from its tear-gas fogs to snatch a riot leader. Ogilvie turned over under water and swam deeper, deeper to where the greenness turned to darkness and his blood drummed up the past. The snatch squad was brave, clean work compared to what he'd done.

He touched mud and dug with his fingers to find a mussel. He thrust off from the mud and rose into the screaming sun. He trod

14

water, turning his face from the sun. On the western side of the gorge from which he had jumped was a cave cut by centuries of floods. In front of the cave was a sloping bank of sandy soil; smudged with the ashes of an old fire on which was set a black cooking pot. Ogilvie threw the mussel with his right hand and it rattled into the cooking pot.

He duck-dived. A boy again. 'Kiltie.' They used to shout that at you in Edinburgh when you were on a pass. Only if you were on your ownio though. They knew better than to shout it at two or more of you. 'Kiltie, kiltie, caul' bum.' Mockery because they knew you didn't have what they had. A family. Only the Institute – the Montrose Military Institute for Boys. Mockery right enough. Aye, and maybe envy because they didn't have what you had. A swank uniform. Five brass buttons down the front with the St Andrew's Cross on them. A Balmoral with the Institute badge. Again the St Andrew's Cross. And the Institute motto: *Vincere aut Perdere Omnia*, To Win or Lose It All. And the kilt. 'Kiltie, kiltie, caul' bum.' And the sporran. 'Keeps his balls in his sporran.'

Ogilvie dug in the mud and found two more mussels. What did he keep in his brain? Rodd. McAskill. Belfast. Ireland. His blood drumming the past, Ogilvie rose again to the screaming sun, a mussel in either hand. He threw with his left hand first. He missed the pot. He threw with his right hand. The mussel went into the pot. He duck-dived again. 'Kiltie, kiltie, caul' bum. Nothing but a wee orphan.'

Ogilvie collected three more mussels in the mud and, after duck-diving again, another two. He swam to the sloping bank of sandy soil and went into the cave. It was furnished with a chrome and plastic table with matching chairs and a bed made from rawhide strips stretched over an iron bedstead. Against the rear wall of the cave was an old cupboard. On a rock shelf were some cans of food, bottles and jars. Ogilvie took a match from a screw-top jar and restarted the fire, using dried flotsam and adding gum branches. The mussels in the pot, he covered with river water and put on the fire.

The smoke of the fire curled up under the overhang of the cave and was trapped there so that no smoke rose to the skyline. Ogilvie positioned the rawhide bed and lay down on it, his head in the smoke, protected from the flies, and his boots in the sun, drying.

He could lie up here for ever, watching the bulled brass glint of the sun on the river and listening to the birds singing. Except they didn't exactly sing. Sort of cheeked each other. Chiacked, Aussies said. A bit like Aussie's themselves. Flat insults first to see what you were made of.

A couple of cockatoos flashed white and gold down the river, cheeking each other all the way. Shug Rodd and himself. Raw recruits, cock-a-doodle-dooing as they lined up for short arm inspection by the doc.

Ogilvie glanced at the pot. The water was boiling. And the mussels were opening up. Like himself. He got up. The tip of a mussel was sticking above the boiling water. He snatched it out of the pot and juggled it from hand to hand to cool it. He ripped the meat from the shell. Not bad grub.

Better than field rations. 'We eat the jungle boots, sir, and wear the field rations.' Part of McAskill's legend, that crack, made to a visiting bigwig in Borneo. Back in the Sixties that would be. Aye, he could be a deadpan wee comic right enough, the same McAskill. Effective with it. After helping to see off the Indonesians in Borneo, his legend put him in a position to raise the Special Independent Counter Insurgency Company. Plenty of volunteers. Not you-you-and-yous either. The real McCoy. And a fair few wanting to extend their service. Like yours truly, Alec Ogilvie. Aye, even if it meant becoming a cowboy.

Ogilvie went back into the cave and fossicked among the bottles on the rock shelf. He found some Worcestershire sauce and doused the next mussel with it. He grinned to himself. Like eating at his own wake after that coffin business.

Vin owed him for the coffin business. Vin would pay his debt. Ogilvie went to the river and drank. Should've kept that can of beer instead of scattering the goats with it.

Something else had scattered them first. He knew what. That bloody dingo. And his own dog who was running with the dingo.

He went back into the cave and from the cupboard took a dingo trap.

5

Des Parkes watched the electric jug boiling. Be a nice change if she blew up. But she wouldn't and his wife Mary was shouting, 'Where's my tea?'

He tugged the cord from the electric jug. 'Coming,' he shouted, and poured boiling water onto his shaving brush in the washbasin. Then he poured the rest onto the teabag in his wife's breakfast cup.

'Want something to eat, darl?' he shouted, adding powdered milk to the tea and stirring it with the handle of his razor while his wife shouted, 'Sometimes I wonder where you are in your mind, Des Parkes. You know I don't have anything to eat until breakfast so why don't you cook me some?'

He picked up the tea. Mary was getting slow. For sure. Last Sunday she had got off a shorter answer to the same question before he'd finished stirring her tea. There again, he had been stirring it with his toothbrush.

Along the upper deck, his bare feet made no sound. He pushed open the door marked 'Bridal Suite' and stepped over the combing, shuffling his false teeth. 'How are you this morning, darl?'

Mary Parkes put *The Australian Women's Weekly* down. She

sighed as she took the cup of tea. 'Bit of a migraine. But all things considered.'

Her head was covered in metal clips attached to her hair. He rubbed the pink patch on his forehead where a skin cancer had been cut out. 'Yeah, you've got a load on your mind, darl. I can see that. Ought to sell you for spares.'

'At least I've got some spares. You're totally clapped out.'

'Right, darl. You're Rolls. Beautiful bodywork. I'm only old Royce, the engine.'

'Funny.' She sipped her tea. 'Very funny.' She sipped again. 'So's this tea.' She took a good swallow. 'I've been letting myself go.' Her hand strayed towards the magazine, then to her face. 'We must do something.'

He rubbed his whiskers. 'You're not wrong, darl. I'll shave. You turn your face inside out.'

The hum of the generator was strong as he went onto the deck again and down the stairs to the main saloon. He opened the cold cupboards, one, two, three. Hardly worth wasting fuel to keep this lot cold. Not enough for a wowser's picnic. Not even enough to make a gnat pee.

Have to check the big cold room. But later. Later.

Up the stairs he went to the wheelhouse. He opened the flag locker, took out the No Grog flag and found behind it a bottle of OP rum. Nothing beat finding a bottle you'd forgotten hiding.

His arm on the wheel to ease the passage of the bottle to his mouth, Des Parkes stared out over the chook run to the ocean of sand beyond the loops of the river.

As the rum hit him, he remembered his Grandpa Jim and the story of him getting into a game of cards on his honeymoon and winning, winning until he won the *River Queen* from her owner, Captain Jeff Allison.

Des Parkes drank to his Grandpa Jim and laughed, spluttering rum. Poor old Captain Jeff must've thought Grandpa Jim wouldn't be able to collect the bet. But Grandpa Jim had sunk eight linked bullock drays into the Murray River and then steered the *River Queen* onto the drays.

A year's haul from the river before he settled Rainbow Downs, his first homestead, the *River Queen*. A mighty man, Grandpa Jim. And not a bad bloke, his own dad, killed diving off the top deck in drunken celebration of the arrival of a son.

Me, thought Des Parkes, surprised, drinking to Grandpa Jim again and then to his dad. A great story for the locals to tell the tourists. Not that there were many of either. Not since the bloody government decided it would be too expensive to add a 50-mile spur of bitumen from the new highway to his pub. Dills. Best tourist attraction this side of Ayers Rock.

Best? Only. Yet the tourist coaches wouldn't risk the track any more. Not since that flaming car-hire company put the black on people using their cars on it. Wasn't his fault those Poms had done their diff. Bloody Poms. Didn't have enough sense to light a fire and wait by a hire vehicle till someone came to look for it and them. Bloody Poms. Trying to make it on foot with what they'd drained from the radiator. And doing a perish the week after he'd got things fixed up. New cabins. New ablution block. New floodlights. New beds. New fencing. Sudan O'Brien's work. And his off-sider Vodka Mahonsky's. Mad as a meat axe, Vodka, but he knew fencing.

Des Parkes held the rum bottle up to the light. Might as well knock her off before someone else found her and knocked her off. Bit like women, bottles. He shuffled his false teeth into a grin and turned from the mirage to the humpies. Outside them, a mob of kids squatted round a camp fire, eating cornflakes from the packet and sucking condensed milk from the tin, while a yelp of dogs fought in the dust for the remains of the TV dinners of the night before. Must order up another batch on the next truck. Pity a man

19

couldn't order up the TV, too. Tourists would make their way along any track for their TV.

Des Parkes took another swig from the rum bottle. The last kid on the condensed milk tin got to his feet and went to an old corrugated-iron water tank lying on its side near the fire. He began beating on the tank with the empty, condensed milk tin.

Des Parkes leaned out of the wheelhouse, roaring, 'Shut up, or I'll have a word with your father.'

The kid kept banging away as he shouted, 'Tell him I want to have a word with him as well.'

Des Parkes withdrew into the wheelhouse. Bobbie bloody Gordon Menzies Maley. Bel's eldest. Cheeky little bastard. But he could ride. Oh, pretty to watch. Bel had horsemen in her. Wasn't only Bobbie. His brother. Harold Holt Maley. One of Bel's jokes that, giving her kids politicians' names. Even her daughter, Enid Lyons Maley. Looking after thirteen kids at the last tally-muster, Bel. Not all hers. Adopted most of them. Well, bush style. Thirteen. No, fourteen. He'd been forgetting Boondoo's kid, Olga.

The canvas water bag, hanging from the wheelhouse ceiling, dripped onto Des Parkes's hand. He trickled water into the rum bottle, swilled it round before drinking and kept his eye on Olga who was carrying Boondoo's didjeridu.

Bobbie grabbed the didjeridu and tried to blow a note on its long, hollowed-out, hardwood stem. All he got was a scream from Olga. He dropped the didjeridu. Olga picked it up and swung it at him. She fell over. Bobbie laughed. Des Parkes grinned.

'Are you there?' Mary Parkes shouted.

Des Parkes put the rum bottle down. 'No, I'm here.'

'Well, that's something, I suppose. Last night you thought you were at a funeral. Supposing the girls had seen you. Morbid. That coffin. That Boondoo droning away on his didjeridu. Someone ought to take an axe to it.'

20

'Have to take an axe to Olga first.'

'Poor little kid. Leave her out of it. Her mum's only been dead a year and that Boondoo acts as if Olga doesn't exist.'

'Boondoo's all right.' Des Parkes grinned. 'He lets Olga look after his didjeridu.'

'You ought to talk to Boondoo.'

'Have.'

'I mean seriously.'

'Right, boss,' said Des Parkes.

That kept her quiet. Always did. Always would. It was what her old man used to say to her mum and Mary didn't like to be reminded of her mum's domineering streak. Des Parkes trickled a little more water into the rum bottle. He had talked to Boondoo. Seriously. One of the most serious conversations he'd ever had with anyone.

Suddenly, he ducked below the level of the wheelhouse panelling. The bastard, Vin Sheean. The dirty, combo bastard. Des Parkes peeked over the edge of the panelling. Vin Sheean, the bastard, easing himself out of the sunshine roof of the old car – the dirty, combo, puzzling bastard. Getting into his big, baggy blue overalls inside the old car with Bel inside there too. What must that be like?

The kids were crowding round Sheean as he made his way towards the long, tin barracks of the Bachelor Quarters, 50 yards away. Sheean was pulling lollies from his pockets to give to the kids. The one who'd been beating on the water tank said something to Sheean, pointing. Definitely Bobbie Gordon Menzies Maley, pointing.

Sheean turned, laughing, yelling, 'I can see you, Des, you perv. I can see you peeping.'

Parkes crouched lower. Combo bastard. If only Bel had him tied with a kid. Yea, a Malcolm Fraser Maley. Parkes risked another peek. Sheean was walking on his hands. Combo clown. The Shire should be charging him and the rest of its single workers to live in the Bachelor Quarters. Not throwing it in as part of the job. Worst sight he had ever seen was that combo turning the old car off the track near the humpies. Trouble. And then Ogilvie marching in a week later from Tim Webster's safari camp to cut out his final check by spending up big. Whisky with beer chasers. And Sheean. More trouble. Nothing worse than a booze artist with a cheque who finds himself a bludging mate with a thirst.

Out on the bridge again, Parkes ran up the No Grog flag – a white towel on which a beer glass had been drawn in red paint and crossed out with creosote. He gave the flagpole a shake and three sparrows flew from their perch on the two-way radio aerial, the other end of which was attached to a length of pipe fixed to the wall of the new ablutions block.

Sheean gave up walking on his hands and began to organise the kids for chasey to get rid of them. Parkes returned to the wheelhouse. If only he could get rid of that combo bastard as easily as he was getting rid of the kids. And Ogilvie. Thought he had when Ogilvie decided to go home and Sheean said he could arrange him a berth on a ship. Off they bloody well went in the old car to Darwin. And Sheean was bloody well back three months later, alone. Then, a month later, Ogilvie marched in again, this time with that lean black bitch, Dustbin, behind him, a darker part of his shadow.

Parkes lifted the water bag off its hook and proceeded to water a row of tomato plants in pots, ranged aft in the wheelhouse. He had better things to be thinking of than Ogilvie and Sheean. One tomato was ripe. Des Parkes plucked it and ate it. Juicy. Mary would be ropeable if she found out. The wheelhouse was already a hothouse to her way of thinking. Not just tomatoes. Nectarines. Peaches. And ferns, she reckoned, to keep the place cool. He could do with cooling himself. That combo bastard Sheean was right. He had been perving. Bel. But he couldn't do anything about it. Not with Mary the way she was now. Streuth, he was supposed to have better things to think of.

Des Parkes rehung the water bag and crossed the wheelhouse to get a better view of the race track. Funny. Tourists were always surprised to find Rainbow had a race track. Especially Poms. As if you could have horses without a race track. And he now had horses. The best.

6

Halliday went forward to the co-pilot's seat of the aircraft. The country was even bigger – and wider – up front. Bigger, wider and drier, dams like rusty nail heads, tacking green patches in place amid the red sand and rocks. He should be walking through that country, not flying over it. Getting the feel of it down through his lungs and up through his feet. The only way. No time. Or not enough. Which came to the same full stop and end it. At least he would be driving part of the way to Tim Webster's safari camp and when he got there it was to be hunting on foot unless what he'd heard about Tim Webster was true.

'Tommy,' Halliday said to the pilot, 'I've heard a lot about this guy Webster.'

'Everything you've heard is true, Tembo,' said Tucker, matching Halliday's use of his nickname. 'My oath it is. Tim Webster's the Best Bloody Bushman in Australia. Shoots buffalo from horseback.'

'How about that?' said Halliday. And thought, Fisi did good to find this guy Webster. If hunting buffs on horseback weren't enough, there were always the crocs. A hungry croc would do.

23

Halliday studied the radar scan, then the air speed indicator, and said to Tucker, 'How long you calculate?'

Tucker said, 'Whistle up a tail wind, Tembo, and we'll make it in a couple of hours. No probs.'

Halliday rested his hands on the dual control stick in front of him. 'Want me to take her for a spell?'

Tucker jerked his head rearwards. 'Only if I can take her.'

'No deal, boy. Adults only. And no more aerobatics.'

'You caught her, didn't you?'

Halliday slapped Tucker on the shoulder and went back to the cabin. OK, he'd caught her. Would be be able to hold her? Not by grabbing and groping. This woman should've been his first and only. She was certainly going to be his last. He sat down and faced her. Only the top button of her shirt was undone. He reached out to undo the second button. She slapped his hand away.

Halliday said, 'Not a sign of last night. You amaze me, Bibi. So sweet down there. So sour up here.'

'I'm remembering you in bed.'

'There I go, Bibi, leading to a counter puncher. Only one thing for it.'

'Yes?'

'I'm going to dictate you out of my life.'

Halliday took a mini-tape-recorder from the side pocket of his safari jacket. He switched on and said, 'A is for Australia, the three-million-square-mile continent . . .'

Of all the cockamamie assignments. Australia A–Z – A new view of the oldest continent by Scott Halliday and Lewis Ashby. God-awful blurb. Godawful project. Yet the deal was worth more than he had made in royalties from his first three books written in blood, sweat, toil and tears. He grinned. Or at least vino, vinegar, oil and adultery. Not to mention those years as a street reporter for the good old International Press Union. The IP, U crap.

Now where was he? What was he? Not a tape-recorder writer. Old street reporter Halliday had forgotten to switch off and the tape was recording only his silence and the roar of the aircraft. He repeated, 'A is for Australia, three-million-square-mile continent where bad Americans go when they are dead but won't lie down.'

He switched off. The hell with it. Talking a book only emphasised the ego incest of the whole literary process. He grinned. Must work that one off on Fisi. Nothing the old hyena liked more than chewing on fresh bull.

The hell with Fisi, too, Australia A–Z was a trick. Australia didn't run from A to Z. A to R for Retarded, maybe. And if Fisi wanted to take it beyond that, well, Fisi would have to write it up from the tapes they'd already done. Then Fisi would be in line for what he really wanted: Tembo Halliday's gut for memoirs. Like the boy crawling around inside the elephant which had won him the nickname Tembo.

'Ever tell you about the drunk elephant I shot up at Lamu in northern Kenya?' he said to Sue Cornwall.

She did not reply and thinking she hadn't heard him because of the engine noise, he raised his voice. 'Ever tell –?'

'Yes, you did,' she said. 'The elephant had been eating doum-palm nuts which fermented in its stomach and you had to shoot it because you wanted the nuts for yourself.'

'Quick, Bibi.'

'But what I couldn't understand was whether the boy you described crawling around inside the elephant was there when you shot it or went in after you shot it.'

'Quick, Bibi. And sharp. So was the boy. He crawled inside the elephant to get himself some tasty bits after it was cut open and gutted.' Halliday grinned. 'Maybe you should know what I did with elephant's balls.'

25

She wouldn't look at him 'You had them for breakfast,' she said, 'and you've been talking nothing else since.'

'Quicker and sharper, Bibi.' He kept grinning. 'What I did was send elephant balls to my first wife who was putting me through the divorce mill. Told her she could have them but not these.'

Sue Cornwall looked at him then. He gripped his crotch with his right hand and shook it up and down. 'Not these, Bibi.'

'Why not?' she said. 'You seem to prefer your tongue and want only mine.'

Halliday's grin was now as savage as the pain it concealed. '*Mimi ni nyama*,' he said. '*Wewe kisu.*'

She had no reply. He translated. 'I am the meat. You are the knife.' But he was talking more to the pain than to her.

7

Mary Parkes sat up in bed and said, 'Des Parkes, what are you doing?'

Halfway out of his football guernsey, Des Parkes said, 'You know I'm the local JP. I've just married us again and we're going to have a second honeymoon.'

'Civil marriages don't count for us.'

'My bloody luck. I married the first female parish priest.'

He took off his shorts and began to fold them before she could tell him to. But she said, 'Those terrible, daggy underpants. There's a hole in the back of them.'

'It would be a sad arse that didn't rejoice after one of your beanfeasts, darl.'

'Des Parkes! You'll be the death of me.'

'You know I'm the local coroner as well. I'll give the cause of death as ultimate ecstasy.'

'Des Parkes!'

'That's me. Your JP for better, your coroner for worse. Now will you take that flaming ironmongery out of your hair? Or do you want me to drag it off with my magnetic donger?'

'Des Parkes! The girls might hear you one of these days.'

'The girls are a thousand miles away, listening to the sisters tell them how to curl their pinkies at ecumenical tea parties.'

She looked at the clock. 'They're at church. And so should we be.'

'Not our fault if the church left us.'

'Had to. You know that. We should leave too. Rainbow's never going to come good.'

'My bloody oath it is. And the church'll be back. The church and the pub go together like St Peter and St Paul. Told Father Ming that when he decided to jack up the church and tow her away.'

Mary Parkes started to take the metal curlers from her hair. 'Yelboom's going ahead. The mine. More people there than here. They need the church. And they need the pub. There, not here.'

'The pub can't be moved again. Rainbow'll come good. You'll see. We've still got the school.'

'But we haven't got the schoolteacher. He went to Yelboom, too. The money. Yelboom's a goer.'

Des Parkes took off his underpants. 'Yelboom my bum. I'll lay you odds she's Yelbust.' He moved to the bed. 'What say we get the girls a little brother?'

'You know we're past it.'

'Speak for yourself, darl. We've got to keep the numbers up. They'll take the flaming school away otherwise.'

'They'll take it away anyway. No teacher. No school.'

'But there is a teacher.'

'There isn't.'

27

'There is. You.'

'That was years ago.'

'The Department don't seem to think so. They want you for interview.'

She threw a handful of metal curlers on the floor, 'You applied for me. Without telling me. I won't do it.'

He got onto the bed beside her. 'Be good for you, darl. Take your mind off yourself.'

She turned away from him. 'You haven't shaved.'

'Clean forgot, darl. You're always on my mind.'

'Sometimes I think you kissed the Blarney stone.'

'She didn't taste as good as you.'

'You've been drinking.'

'That's me, darl. One Sunday pleasure after another.'

8

Vin Sheean had not seen his face in the toecaps of a pair of army boots before. He stared at himself. As in a glass darkly. No, as in a pair of spoons ebony. Two faces, bulbous in the sunlight streaming through the windows and open door of the Bachelor Quarters. Two faces shifting. 'So am I,' Sheean said aloud to himself. 'So am I.'

The money he had taken from the boots lay on the concrete floor with a pair of clean khaki socks and a pair of rolled-up puttees. Before replacing the socks and puttees in the boots he gave them a final polish with the socks. The money he shoved into a side pocket of his overalls. Three fifty at least. He replaced the boots, under Ogilvie's bed, exactly aligned as they had been.

The corrugated iron of the Bachelor Quarters creaked, expanding in the heat. Sheean turned towards the door, his mouth dry with sudden guilt. From the canvas water bag, hanging sweating in the doorway, he poured water into the enamel mug which was tied to the water bag.

The enamel mug he raised two-handed. The cup of damnation. He drank. Salty. Sweat of poor old Og's brow. Sheean closed his eyes and opened them as quickly again; the past was harsher than the glare of the sunlight. How many widow's mites in the first lot he'd stolen?

Truth is beauty. He'd give old Aquinas T. an argument on that proposition. But would Aquinas T. be able to give him an argument on the proposition: men are fated to repeat themselves to show what they did the first time was wrong?

The money felt good, though. Leaves for a nest in one of those communes in Queensland. Anywhere. Away. Bel was closing in, surrounding him with herself and her kids. Pity she hadn't taken a fancy to old Ogilvie. But he lived as if he didn't know what women were for.

Sheean peered out of the doorway. It was Og more than Bel who had him worried. Og was mad. The poetry. The funeral business when he got drunk. The slow marching. The drill for resting on arms reversed. And the way the past pumped out of him. Yes, pumped. Like arterial blood from a dying man. Sheean shivered.

Water dripped from the enamel mug as it swung on its string. Sheean knew he definitely had to get away. He had the feeling Ogilvie was going to tell him something he could not take. Some people did that. Left the worst to last. He had the feeling Ogilvie was one of them and the only cure for the feeling was distance. The plane tomorrow. Then a nice nest in a nice hippy commune, deep in the rainforest where nothing stirred except a wooden spoon in a vegetable stew. Might even try meditation and pot. Jesuit style. Not Dominican.

Sheean put out his hand to stop the pendulum mug. The Dominican: 'Reverend Father, may I smoke while meditating?' Superior: 'Most certainly not.' The Jesuit: 'Reverend Father, may I meditate while smoking?' Superior: 'Of course, of course.'

Sheean went back to Ogilvie's boots and adjusted them a fraction. Yes, a little pot for his mind's sake. He would need it, wondering whether Og was going to track him down. Sheean went back to the doorway and peered out again. And yet if it hadn't been for Og wading in the night of the fight, Des Parkes would've been pointing to another bloodstain on the pub floor and telling the world Vin Sheean had got no more than he deserved, insulting a camper van full of miners on a roo–shooting spree.

Sheean stepped into the sun. It'd been good at first to have a mate like Og. Less conspicuous. A man on his own in the Outback was a puzzle to solve. A man and his mate were part of the landscape. The solution to it.

9

Ogilvie rubbed his hands with fresh gum leaves grabbed from a tree growing from the gorge side. Then he rubbed the dingo trap to kill his smell on it. He hammered the long steel peg which anchored the trap into the ground with a chunk of rock and covered the peg and its chain with sand and gum leaves. He spread the trap's jaws, their steel teeth filed down so as not to cut through the leg of any animal giving it a chance to escape. He drifted more sand and gum leaves over the trap itself.

The leftover cooked mussels were worth a try. He placed the mussels as bait between the trap and the wall of the gorge. In front of the trap, he laid a dry branch to make sure the dingo would lift his foot onto the trap plate and spring it.

Ogilvie walked backwards, brushing his footmarks away from near the trap.

Dingos were scavengers. Chances were it would come sniffing round the old camp. Ogilvie picked up the chunk of rock he had used to hammer the peg. What if it wasn't the dingo but his own dog came sniffing? Ogilvie threw the chunk of rock. It hit the trap plate and the trap snapped shut.

Ogilvie looked up. Admit it. He didn't want to catch anything. Anyone. He never wanted to see anyone caught helpless again, eyes sending an appeal.

The strip of blue sky above Ogilvie had ragged edges, ripped by the shadowed edges of the gorge.

A flag. And music, music echoing off tenement walls. The Pipes and Drums of the Montrose Military Institute for Boys exercising its right to collect funds by parading through the town.

Music. The Institute's march. 'Hielan' Laddie.' The jingling of coins, thrown into a grey army blanket held by a section of cadets.

In front of the section, the Institute's Pipes and Drums led by Sammy Abercrombie, throwing his mace fish silvery into the air. Behind Sammy, Bully Beef Sammy, yours truly, Mascot Corporal Alec Ogilvie with Bran, the wolfhound. Bully Beef Sammy was the boy. Twenty slices of bread and beef in his belly. Ration slices, won the night before at illegal pontoon by the light of a candle. Bully Beef Sammy, first on the Institute's barracks square after reveille. First to swot up the history of the Institute and recite it.

Ogilvie tried to throw the memory away with the used gum leaves. But his lips moved with the memory of Bully Beef Sammy. 'The Montrose Military Institute for Boys was originally founded by an anonymous admirer of James Graham, Marquis of Montrose, born 1612, died 1650, for the benefit of the orphans of his Scots and Irish soldiers . . .'

Ogilvie pulled himself a handful of fresh gum leaves. Not a bad

31

soldier, Bully Beef Sammy. Made colour sergeant. And nobody's fool when it came to looking after Number One. Bought himself out of the Army to run his own dance band as soon as he heard what was happening to the Regiment. Poor old Sammy, killed in a dance-hall rammy.

The scent of the fresh gum leaves came to Ogilvie as he rubbed them on his hands. Music. Different music. Ambulances hee-hawing down the old, brave music of the pipes and drums. The rattle of dustbin lids. The roar of armoured personnel carriers – the pigs. The pigs roaring and the dustbin lids rattling in Belfast and out to the bandit country beyond.

Still rubbing his hands with the gum leaves, Ogilvie went back to the trap. Should've bought himself out same as Sammy Abercrombie and run . . . What?

For his life. As it was he'd found himself with a can he couldn't carry. A can of scrambled brains. Rodd's brains, scrambled by McAskill. Aye, with a wee bit of help from your truly, 621, Trooper Ogilvie, A.

Rodd hadn't bought himself out either. When he'd heard about the Regiment, he did a vanish into Ireland and the roughest game going.

Carefully, Ogilvie reset the trap. Rodd'd done a vanish with the ghosts of his grandfather and his father who'd also served in the Regiment. Had spoken for them and for himself to yours truly at Sammy Abercrombie's farewell booze-up. 'We've tried shaming them, the English, into decency by loyalty. Even starving ourselves at their doors. But shame's not in them where we're concerned. So, we've got to do for ourselves what they trained us to do so well for them – fight.'

This time, Ogilvie didn't brush his footprints from round the trap. Big-hearted Alec, he thought, giving a dog a chance his old mucker Rodd hadn't had. The chance to see something was off. A danger sign. Even Judas had done that for Christ.

32

Wayne Donaldson had a chew at the end of his long fair moustache. His big hands and brawny forearms absorbed the judder of the prime-mover steering wheel into his chest. He knew he was driving too fast and had been driving too long. It was the pills. They made him feel like he was the prime-mover. All working muscle. None of your body-builder balloons. Unstoppable. The 270 Brake Horse-power Man. He slammed into a gear change. The two-trailer road-train linked to the prime-mover swayed, its load of sheep too tightly packed to move.

The track thundered ahead of him in a crisscross of sandy ruts and stony corrugations. It dipped and at the bottom of the dip was a white post, numbered to show flood levels. Near the post lay a heavy-duty tyre, its outer casing stripped from it by the pounding grind of the track.

Donaldson felt his wheels begin to drift in deeper sand, corrected and rewarded himself with another pill washed down with the last of the beer in the can he was drinking. He threw the can out of the window. Might be a beer-can tree growing for the return trip. Seriously. No more beer. No more pills. He had enough gee to take him to Sweetwater Station.

Three hundred yards ahead, the track vanished in a flooding, blue mirage and Donaldson tried to imagine the sweat running down from his bald head to his face was the first trickle from the cold shower at Sweetwater. Bloody hope. Still, when he made it to Sweetwater, there would be a wad of the no-questions-asked, another instalment for the bludgers who were on his back.

Jeez, he must've been the original dill to believe the urger who said he would be his own boss at twenty-five. Here he was, bald at thirty-two geed on pills and piss, and he seemed to owe more than when he first bought his rig on that special, low-deposit, pay-as-you-earn, hire-purchase deal. Unbeatable terms, according to the urger. Unbeatable was right. He would be paying his age pension to the finance company the way the arrears were already piling up and the way they were chasing him. He switched on the radio. A snatch of news he didn't want. Then a disc jockey, talking about golden oldies and the Beatles.

'What do you mean, golden oldies, you fuckwit?' Donaldson shouted. 'I saw the Beatles myself when they were here on their big tour.'

The disc jockey ignored him although Donaldson could see him quite clearly, a skinny bloke with swept-back hair and a velvet jacket over a white skivvy.

The sound of 'A Hard Day's Night' filled the prime-mover cab. Donaldson shouted at the disc jockey, 'You trying to say I'm an oldie? I'll drop you, you poofdah fuckwit, if you say another word.'

Donaldson began trying to synchronise his gear changes to the beat of 'A Hard Day's Night'.

When the disc jockey spoke again, Donaldson shouted, 'I warned you, you poofdah fuckwit.'

And his foot went down harder on the accelerator. The track roared ahead, endless, empty except for the succession of mirages which kept leaping ahead of Donaldson's prime-mover as he drove it towards them.

Ashby swiped at the flies on his face with his new gaberdine hat and the flies joined the others on the back of his white tennis shirt. This is it, Ashby thought, the fabled Middle of Nowhere, lightly disguised as a place called Paradise Creek. He should induce Tembo to include such names in the book. Under H for Humour perhaps. Or even I for Irony. True, there was a creek. But no water. And what about Paradise? Surely not the airstrip? It was no more than a change of nuance in a landscape where grey modulated into purple.

He sneaked a look at the man squatting to his right and slightly in front of him. A beefy old party in a big brown hat, blue shirt, dusty white trousers and brown, elastic-sided boots. Dried beefy. Too much sun which hadn't reduced his paunch. Like a camel's hump, to get him through dry spells?

Ashby raised one of the cameras which were slung around his neck and knocked off a shot of Tim Webster, who didn't look round.

Self-sufficient old party. Ashby swiped at the flies again. Nevertheless. Nevertheless. He had been fantastically lucky to catch up with this self-sufficient old party after Tembo heard the name Tim Webster mentioned across a crowded bar in Sydney as the Best Bloody Bushman in Australia.

Ashby snorted at a fly trying to crawl up his nose. The Gofer of the Year Award to Harold Ashby. Of the Year? Of the Decade? To find Webster he had to find the Best Bloody Bush Pilot in a country full of Best Bloodies. He had. Lindsay Tucker. Known as Tommy. Nicknames here had a ponderous inevitability. Another subject for Tembo? He was after all an expert on nicknames. As who knew better? Fisi. Ashby grimaced in disgust.

35

'You all right?' said Tim Webster.

'Sure,' said Ashby, 'sure,' and then, to cover his embarrassment at being caught making faces – and muttering? – by someone he thought was looking elsewhere, added, 'Have you any fly repellent in your vehicle, Tim?'

Webster shook his head and stood up. 'Can let you have a shotgun,' he said. 'But the best thing – no bullshit – is let your whiskers grow and the buggers impale themselves.' Webster scratched his own whiskers. His lips moved fractionally. A grin? Or just his hand moving his face? Ashby couldn't tell.

Lewis, thought Ashby. Australians made such a thing of first names. Yet Webster after – my God, was it three days? – Webster still had to call him Lewis. Was there protocol, a proper interval? Here in the fabled Middle of Nowhere? Had he failed to observe Outback protocol by calling Webster, Tim, prematurely?

Tucker had insisted on being called Tommy immediately. Pity about the poor boy's teeth. Nothing wrong with his IQ. The way he used the radio transceiver net to track Tim Webster, camped here on the way north to his safari camp.

Ashby touched his instant camera. He had got a good shot of Tommy before takeoff on their flight to meet Webster. Tembo should have come, too. Otherwise engaged with that floozie, Suzie. Ashby grimaced in disgust again, caught himself at it and glanced at Webster to see whether he had noticed. He hadn't. He was squatting once more, gazing south.

Ashby thought about getting another shot of Webster. Instant? He shook his head. He had already tried instant and Webster hadn't been impressed by the magic.

Tommy had been impressed. So delighted he had flown straight back to get Tembo after Tim Webster had agreed to take on the job.

Pure magic, thought Ashby. Not quite pure perhaps. Tembo Halliday's money helped. And his name.

36

Tim Webster glanced to his left at his white-painted four-wheel drive. Silly. He knew it was. But he couldn't restrain his pride every time he saw his name on the side of the four-wheel drive and the name of his company: Ausafaris Proprietary Limited.

Well, it beat droving, poking a mob along all day, trying to keep a bit of condition on them, lullabying them at night in case they might rush. How many miles? How many years? How many head? Too bloody many. This was the life. His eyes shifted to Ashby. Queer coot. The way he sneaked looks at a man. And that whippet face of his. The way he muttered sometimes. And took flaming photos all the time. You would think he didn't have a memory. Flyweight. Yeah, the way he kept hitting the flies with his hat, that would be right. Maybe he should use a handbag. Webster's mouth moved fractionally. What was it that big Scots bastard, Ogilvie, used to say about small blokes? 'Two pound heavier than a gas mantle.' Not a bad big bastard, Ogilvie. But he had to go. No hard feelings. Just as well. A man got to a certain age and if he didn't know who could drop him in a fair fight and who couldn't, he wasn't going to get any older.

Webster stood up and his legs creaked. Like an old saddle, he thought and said, 'Drink?'

Ashby rubbed the tennis sweatband he had on his wrist against his forehead. 'I don't drink.'

'Water, I meant.'

'I have my own.'

To make sure, Ashby touched the metal canteen attached to his webbing belt. Webster nodded and grinned. With the canteen and all those cameras dangling from him, he looked like a Japanese Christmas tree. Only the camera with the long lens was more like an old Lewis gun.

Webster went to his four-wheel drive and lifted the canvas water bag from the front bull bar. He took a single swig of the tar-tasting

37

water, rinsed it around in his mouth before swallowing and replacing the water bag on its leather back pad.

Slow. Slow. The only way. This bloke Ashby ran around as if he'd forgotten to shake the centipedes from his lairy, white shoes and kept waving a calendar watch that seemed to be too big for his wrist.

Ashby shouted, 'Time?'

Webster dug under the lee of his paunch and took his watch from its leather belt pouch. 'Only nine,' he said. 'And it's Sunday.'

Ashby said, 'I know what day it is, thank you. But their ETA was eight.'

'Time's the only thing there's plenty of up here.'

'Perhaps. It's just . . .'

Ashby's reply tailed off into the fly hum and the remembered growl of Tembo Halliday the first occasion they met.

'Son, to be fustest and bestest, a writer's got to be faster than the pen slinger who writes better and better than the pen slinger who writes faster.'

Halliday in his betrophied apartment where all the rugs had animal heads and the chair at the writing desk was put together from kudu horns and rhino hide. Halliday was no longer bestest and fustest. Finicky when he wasn't near incoherent. And no more 'Son', 'Fisi' now.

Webster watched Ashby muttering; wondered whether he was going troppo; decided he'd been born troppo and said, 'No bullshit, I almost couldn't believe it when you said Tembo Halliday wanted to use my camp for his base. I've been a fan of his for years.'

'So you said.'

'No bullshit. I've read everything he's ever written, especially the African stuff.'

'Especially the African stuff?'

'Well, I was there myself for a while. North. The Tigers were –'

38

'Tigers? In Africa?'

'Tanks.'

'Oh, Tembo will be impressed. He loves to chew over old wars.'

'He has been in a fair few.'

'Absolutely. They daren't start Word War Three until he has his syndication deal sewn up.'

Webster took the makings from his shirt and rolled himself a cigarette. Sarcastic bastard. No reason for him to sneer. Not that you could really tell. Permanent bloody sneer. He lit the cigarette.

'There they are,' he said, 'Mr Ashby.'

Ashby scanned the sky to the south. 'I can't see anything.'

'Listen.'

The drone of aircraft engines gradually jammed the hum of the flies.

'Got it,' said Ashby, putting his long-lens camera to his shoulder. Ought to get an AA mounting for it, thought Webster, catching sight of the aircraft as it turned for its approach to the bush landing strip.

Ashby's camera clicked and whirred. He said, 'Shouldn't you light a fire? Smoke. For wind direction.'

Webster moved towards the four-wheel drive. 'Out here? In this dry? I've got some smoke canisters.' He opened one of the metal boxes on the roof rack of the four-wheel drive and took out two cylindrical smoke flares. 'You take one. Over there. Fifty yards. Pull the tab.'

Ashby ignored him so Webster pulled the tab on his own smoke flare and a column of smoke sputtered and started to drift towards the west. Ashby continued to take pictures.

'Wouldn't it?' said Webster. He jammed the smoke canister into the ground. He took the other and trotted east on long, thin legs, a horseman still, hobbled by his own saddle muscles.

39

12

Using a stick, Boondoo eased the goanna from the campfire by which he was hunkered, near the racetrack. He let the goanna cool a bit before ripping off its tail and throwing the rest to the crows and the ants. He peeled the burnt skin from the tail and bit into the white meat. Number One Bush Tucker. Only cure for a hangover. He flicked the scraps of burnt skin from his fingers into the camp fire and took a sup of sugarless, milkless tea.

He looked towards his stable which leant against a grey, dead gum tree and let out a sudden cooee. Two crows, sidling towards the goanna, took flight and then returned to their feast.

Boondoo bit off another chunk of tail. A man must be mad. But he couldn't've raised a cooee last night after the funeral party when he got back to find his horse Myall being galloped in the moonlight on the race track. He could only watch and realise there was someone better on Myall than he was, Bel's kid, Bobbie.

Boondoo chewed the goanna meat, sluiced it down with tea and belched as he stood up to walk across to his stable, a brushwood and pole construction, stayed to the gum tree with fencing wire.

Inside the stable, Myall, the blaze on his forehead a star shining in the darkness, spoke first to Boondoo. He took off his white jockey cap and rubbed the racing saddle balanced on the side of Myall's stall. Under his bright green shirt, sweat collected along the line of his money belt.

'Maybe if I could save as quick as you run,' Boondoo said.

Myall whinnied. Boondoo said, 'Aw, look, mate. I only had a couple.'

He moved to Lubra's stall. No way he should be spending money on grog. He needed every cent for the idea. But Ogilvie was a mate. And when your mate got sad shickered, you couldn't stand around

40

allersame a tourist staring at kuri people camped in a creek bed. Tourists. Their fat white legs. Enough to put a man off witchetty grubs. Enough to send a man blind-stabbing out of the Alice into the desert with a flagon, a quart pot and a trannie.

Lubra spoke to him. Boondoo clicked his tongue at her, running his dark hand over her dark flank. Myall stamped in his stall, ready for another gallop.

'Easy, bubba,' said Boondoo. 'You've had all the exercise you need. Me and Lubra take a walk by and by.'

His fingers found the scar pucker high on Lubra's neck, her only brand. Boondoo moved across to Myall and rubbed the star on his forehead. 'Pretty little fella,' he said, and when the colt nuzzled his hand, 'Pretty as a picture.'

The picture Boondoo had was the miracle of Myall being dropped alive though Lubra had a heavy rifle slug in her. Myall being licked to his feet in the rough circle of dead wild horses shot down around a water hole because they were eating out feed needed for cattle.

Boondoo took a crust from his pocket and gave it to Myall. Boondoo himself could taste the memory of horseflesh.

He took a sup of his tea, trying to wash the memory away. And pulled a face. Horseflesh, cut from the rump of one of the carcases, with a glass knife broken from the flagon, and cooked in a satchel of horsehide till the hide was charred. First and last time. He knew kuri people who wouldn't have a bar of roo meat because roos were special to them. Or turtle meat. After the miracle of Myall, he couldn't come at horseflesh. Horses were special to him. But he'd needed that feed to dig the slug out of Lubra with the glass knife, cleaning the wound with his quart pot of water boiled on a fire started by using the flagon bottom as a burning glass. Lubra'd recovered. And so'd he, hunting in the old way, eating in the old way and drinking in the old way. Water. Funny thing. He'd kept

41

listening to the trannie. Music. Mostly country. All the yabber was too much. Except the Melbourne Cup. Listening to the Cup and looking at Lubra and Myall and thinking how he'd found them made the idea come into his head and grow and grow as he rode Lubra, water hole by water hole, out of the desert with Myall following. By the time they got to Rainbow, the idea filled his head.

Now Lubra whinnied. Boondoo began banging his head against the king post, trying to kill the idea. Humbug. He didn't own Myall. He didn't own Lubra. No more. No more. And he didn't know what he could do except pretend he did.

Plurry grog. A man got so far and it pulled him back. She'd always said that. Trish, his wife, Olga's mumma'd always said that. Boondoo kept banging his head against the king post. Trish'd always said the grog wasn't a tongue thirst or a belly thirst. It was a brain thirst. He banged his head even harder. The idea would not go away. Not after Bel's kid, Bobbie. Wasn't a horse in Australia, wasn't a horse in the world could match Myall with Bobbie Maley riding him.

13

Ogilvie eased the coffin up so that it was balanced on his shoulder. He squinted at the sun. Have to get a juldee on. By the right, quick march.

The edge of the coffin bit into his neck where it met his shoulder. The edge of his hand in a killing stroke. The coffin lid rattled against its loose screws. A drum tap. His right hand shifted to keep the coffin balanced as he climbed a wave of sand and passed into the broken shade provided by four new corrugated-iron houses set in a square on a raft of concrete.

He walked from house to house. Not enough room in them to swing a mouse, let alone a cat. And hot. He put the coffin down and fetched a couple of bundles of brushwood from the pile he had collected in the middle of the raft. Up the ladder leaning against the side of one of the houses he went and laid the brushwood lengthways beside those already there. Down and up, he went. Down and up, laying the brushwood all along the roof, covering it. Then he took lengths of rawhide he had prepared. He laid the rawhide over the brushwood in a net pattern. To the ends of the rawhide, he tied stones to hold the brushwood down on the roof. He went inside one of the houses not yet covered. Hot enough to bake a loaf in. He went inside the house he had been working on. Definitely cooler. Bel would notice. Nobody's fool, Bel. She'd told those government people from Down Below where to get off when they tried to force her out of her humpies. She'd move when she was good and ready. Maybe he should tell her about Vin.

Ogilvie went to the standpipe which stuck out of the middle of the concrete raft and turned on the tap. Not a drop. Have to connect it up. Everything else was connected. Vin. If Vin scarpered, he would find him. Done it once. Do it again. Big country. Big. But not enough people in it to hide Vin. Or to get away from thinking about Rodd. His old mucker.

Ogilvie swung his boot at the coffin. The wood cracked and splintered. A door at dawn. He bent down and got the coffin onto his shoulder again. The pub floated in the distance, yellow and blue and green and orange. A fiend with the paint, Des, an absolute fiend. Should've been a sergeant major, Des. If it moves, salute it. If it doesn't, paint it.

Ogilvie marched to the sound of the coffin lid tapping, his old, black boots scrunching on the track, marched on under a timber arch on which was painted in yellow and blue and green and orange:

43

WELCOME TO RAINBOW – MAWGU SHIRE
SHIRE AREA – 54,000 SQUARE MILES
SHIRE POPULATION – 280
SHIRE INDUSTRY – CATTLE

Ogilvie began to sing. He sang 'Pack Up Your Troubles In Your Old Kit Bag'. He sang 'It's A Long Way To Tipperary'. And he sang,

> 'Oh, ye'll take the high road
> An' I'll take the low road,
> An' I'll be in Scotland afore ye ...'

Under the tan of his right arm was a long, bruiselike mark, reddish and blue.

14

Webster would have recognised Tembo Halliday anywhere. The shock of white hair. The long, thin, black cigar sticking out of his mouth like a fuse on a pink, weather-beaten bomb. When Ashby introduced them, Halliday said, 'Nothing wrong with my eyes, Fisi.' He gripped Webster's hand as though it were a gun butt. 'Great to meet you, Tim. Still bringing down those buffs from a horse, Comanche style?'

'There's a chopper available if you prefer, Mr Halliday.'

'No chopper. Saw enough goddamn choppers in Vietnam to last me a lifetime. It's Comanche style for me same as you.'

'Wouldn't know about Comanche, Mr Halliday.'

'Hell, nobody calls me that except my wife's lawyers. Sons of

44

bitches. They know I would smack them in the mouth for calling me anything else. But Tembo's the name to you.'

Webster led the way towards the four-wheel drive. 'I wouldn't really know about Comanches, Tembo. All I do is get on a good horse.'

'The horse squeeze the trigger, eh?'

'No, I do that. When I'm lucky I drop them with a spine shot.'

Halliday halted and gripped Webster's arm. 'You spine-shoot buffalo?'

Webster stared at Halliday's hand. Big hand. Big bloke. Need a cut lunch and a water bag to go round him. Halliday released his grip. 'Spine-shooting. Can't say I'm crazy about it.'

Webster glanced at Ashby who had joined them and said, 'Only way, Tembo. Kill a buffalo outright and she rots on the flat while you're chasing up another one. Spine-shoot the bastards and you can kill them later when you're ready to skin them for the freezer. The Germans want their buffalo meat fresh.'

Halliday said, 'You shoot buffalo meat for the Krauts?'

'They love it, Tembo. Pay well, too. We fly it out.'

'Goddamnit, Tim. Krauts want spine-shot buffalo meat, let them shoot it themselves. Spine-shooting's about their speed.'

Ashby said, 'Tim knows about their speed. He fought them in North Africa. When would that have been, Tim? About '41 or '42?' He laughed.

'Forty-one,' said Webster, 'Tobruk.'

Halliday's shove set Ashby reeling, and Halliday shouted, 'Fisi, you're going to needle yourself into a situation you can't laugh yourself out of one day. So why don't you get the gear off the plane and stowed?'

'Jeez,' said Webster. He had seen Sue Cornwall jump from the aircraft wing to the flat. 'Nobody told me a sheila was coming.'

Halliday said, 'Only round the mountain, Tim.'

45

'Aw, fair enough. If she's going back.'

Ashby on his way to the plane said, 'Might be better at that, Tembo.'

Halliday said, 'Bibi wouldn't want to go home – even if she knew where we were.'

Tim Webster squatted in the dust. 'I'll draw you a mud map.' He smoothed the dust with a sweep of his hand and with his finger drew a line running south to north. 'Here's the track we're on. Back along it five hours and you hit the bitumen.' He extended the line north. 'This is the way we're headed.' He made a cross. 'We strike the bitumen here. About eight hours northwest and we're at my place.'

'That's what I want to see,' said Halliday. 'Heard a lot about it.'

Webster drew a line curving easterly off the highway. 'Thought we might overnight in Rainbow first. Have a few beers. Bit of tucker.'

'All of me,' said Tucker, not for the first time, dumping a big duffel bag on the flat. 'Why not take all of me?'

'Seriously,' Webster said to Sue Cornwall, 'Rainbow's rough as guts. Maybe you would be better home.'

'Be happy to fly you back home,' said Tucker. 'No extra charge.'

His snaggletooth grin vanished into solemn appeal as Sue Cornwall shook her head.

'In that case.' Tucker shook hands all round and loped towards the plane.

Watching him taxiing into the wind for takeoff, Sue Cornwall thought. Home? The flat in London where she'd sat reading magazines about turning a flat into a self-contained pleasure pad. Home? The unit Mum and Dad bought themselves after selling the deep-verandahed house in Sydney where she'd been brought up. Not born. Mum's and Dad's reluctance to have a child born at home anticipated their dying pen with its pearl-grey walls, pearl-grey carpets, pearl-grey drapes and Spanish arches. She'd told Halliday

46

about it once to fill a scary silence, wondering if other women did this, too. He'd guffawed and said, 'Sounds as if Spain has made good its claim to Australia. *Viva muerte.* Long live death.'

Again she felt that Halliday was reading her mind. For he put his arm around her shoulders and moved towards the four-wheel drive. On the roof rack Ashby was stowing their gear. Halliday freed her with a kiss and said to Ashby, 'My rifle.'

Ashby climbed down from the roof rack and got Halliday's rifle from where it was stowed in a spring rack with Webster's in the back of the four-wheel drive. Halliday took the rifle from Ashby, checked it and said, 'Ammo – unless you expect me to use film.'

Ashby's nostrils quivered a comment. From the back of the four-wheel drive, he got a box of ammunition and held it as Halliday loaded his rifle. Halliday then put a handful of rounds into a pocket of his safari jacket.

'Here, Bibi,' he said. She came to him. 'For luck,' he said. And inserted sixteen rounds from the box into the loops on her black belt. He stepped back. 'Serendipity,' he said, 'I love it.'

He emptied the rest of the box into the pockets of his safari jacket. Ashby dropped the empty box and it blew in the wind of Tucker's low-level pass over the four-wheel drive. When he banked to make the return pass, Halliday raised his rifle, led the aircraft and squeezed off a shot.

'Bloody hell,' said Webster, 'You could've hit him.'

'I hit what I want to hit,' said Halliday, 'I miss what I want to miss.'

'Yeah, but you haven't shot your rifle in. Your 'scope could be out of whack.'

Halliday glanced at the ammunition box now about 50 yards away. He raised his rifle and fired. The round pierced the ammunition box dead centre.

'Rock solid, this 'scope,' said Halliday, and when Webster made a face of reluctant agreement, Halliday continued, 'That looks like another but coming on, Tim. People who hire out with me but me no buts.' He opened the door of the four-wheel drive and ushered Sue Cornwall onto the front bench seat. 'Do they, Bibi?'

She ignored him, watching Tucker's aircraft climb into the blue sky. Halliday got in alongside her. Ashby got in the back. Webster climbed into the driver's seat as if into a saddle. He eyed the rifle Halliday now held up right between his legs. 'Safety on?' Webster said.

Halliday roared, 'Do I look like the kind of jerk who rides shotgun with the safety off?'

Webster shook his head and started the engine. The way this Tembo Halliday'd leant into his shot had shown him to be someone who knew guns all right. Firing at an aircraft in flight showed he was trigger happy. A bad, bloody combination.

'Well, do I?' Halliday roared again.

'Just wondering,' said Webster, reversing the four-wheel drive onto the track and then heading north.

Halliday squinted up at the blue sky to where a wedgetail eagle was riding a thermal. Lifting the sun to its killing height, thought Halliday. So Webster hadn't been impressed by his firing at the aircraft. What would he think were he told Tembo Halliday'd had the sudden conviction as he aimed his rifle that he could fire his pain at the aircraft. And that if he'd hit it instead of missing it, the pain would've gone?

15

Mary Parkes did not have anything to wear so she dusted the china cabinet with her old dress while she worked out what she should do.

Amazing how shiny the cabinet became when two weeks' coating of dust was rubbed off the glass and the oak grain of the cabinet caught the sun filtering through the lace curtains she had made specially for the parlour portholes which stared out over the ocean of sand.

She opened the cabinet and took out a sugar bowl, part of the tea set given her as a wedding present by her cousin Delia who had married the dentist and had wanted her to marry his partner.

'He really is rapt, Mary. Just think of the double wedding we could have. Two teachers. Two dentists. The choir. Everything.'

The sugar bowl was cold when Mary Parkes fitted it over her breast. The pansies on it reminded her of faces. Des's face, his eyes sunken in shadow from the bucks' turn of the night before and his black moustache drooping as he turned to watch her coming down the aisle.

All dressed in china. Mary Parkes moved the sugar bowl to the other side where there was no breast, only, and strangely, a stronger memory of her children sucking.

She moved the sugar bowl again, holding it under her chin as the tears ran down her cheeks into it.

'Oh, Mary,' she whispered, yet not speaking to herself for she continued, 'conceived without sin, pray for us who have recourse to thee.'

She put the sugar bowl back in the cabinet and tiptoed down the for'ard stairs, thumbing her yellow panties over her bottom as if suddenly conscious she was being watched. She went into the cabin Des used for his store: saddles and saddle cloths and bridles and bits and plaid cowboy shirts and the good, old Crimean blue and big hats and black and brown, elastic-sided boots and tobacco and knives and socks and billycans and jeans and hammers and axes and bow saws and cartridges and pliers and herself saying to Delia of the dentist, 'I couldn't. Not even if he gave me laughing gas first.'

She could still smile through a sigh at that, the wire hangers on the frock rack jingling. The third frock she tried on was a perfect fit. Blue was not her colour, though. She moved along the rack.

Amazing how good old Des's taste had become. She tugged out a red shirtwaister and held it against herself, breathing in.

Ah, there it was. She put the red shirtwaister back on the rack and slipped the apple-green cotton over her head, smoothing it down and her black hair.

Better. Mary Parkes looked at herself in the mirror. She tied the belt of the apple-green, shook her head, untied the belt and drew it from its loops. She pulled her hair into a pony tail and tied it with the belt. Much better. She smiled and went to the far end of the storeroom where a refrigerator hummed in tune with a wandering blowfly.

The big box of assorted lipsticks was behind the chocolates. She fossicked in the box and withdrew a handful of lipsticks, holding them up to read the names: 'First Kiss', 'Temptation', 'Fever', 'Baby Doll' and . . . Mary Parkes smiled.

Rolling the lipstick she had chosen between her hands to warm it up, she went back to the mirror.

Much, much better, especially with visitors expected. She smiled again, her lips red with 'Lady Rose'.

Would Maureen Staples ever be sick when she returned from Bali full of boasts and colour slides to find that the famous author Tembo Halliday had been through Rainbow on his way to Tim Webster's place?

Served Maureen Staples right for big noting herself. Bali, for heaven's sake. And Japan three years ago. Maureen Staples was only the wife of a station manager, yet she behaved as if her little Graham owned every square mile of Rainbow Downs, Leprechaun Springs and Crock of Gold Creek instead of running it for the new mob from Hong Kong.

Des's by rights. At least Rainbow Downs was, except Des's Grandpa Jim discovered that the shortest distance between two points was from the bank to the pub. Trouble was he owned the pub, not the bank. Died in it. Dear old bloke. All he had at the finish. Poor Des. He hadn't said but she knew why he was so worked up about Tembo Halliday's visit.

Mary Parkes grimaced into the mirror and added a touch of lipstick to the corners of her mouth. She turned. Bel Maley was gazing at her through one of the storeroom portholes. Mary Parkes opened the storeroom door and shouted, 'Go away. Don't you know it's Sunday?'

Bel moved to the door. 'Maybe I need a nice frock too.'

'But it's Sunday,' said Mary Parkes.

Bel came through the door. 'I don't want a Sunday frock.'

She laid a handful of crumpled notes and loose change on the counter and moved to the rack. Mary Parkes followed her. 'All right. Just tell me the kind of frock you want.'

'White.'

'They're all white.'

Bel tugged an orange and blue frock, 'This white?'

Mary Parkes took the dress from her and replaced it on the rack. 'I meant they're all white style. Fashionable.'

Bel continued to examine the rack of frocks. 'I mean colour white,' she said. 'Allersame wedding.' She took from the rack a long frock, all shining and wide-skirted. 'This one. How much?'

'It's not very sensible. Shows the dirt.'

'How much?'

Mary Parkes fingered the money on the counter as though it were dirty washing. 'You haven't got enough, I'm afraid.'

Bel said, 'Lay by. Pay you the rest later.'

'When?'

'One day.'

51

'But who is he? Your fiancé?'

'Fiancé?'

'Your husband-to-be. The man you're going to marry.'

Bel picked up one of the lipsticks, drew a red line on the back of her hand with it, shook her head and replaced the lipstick. 'All my kids. None getting learnt at school no more.'

'Taught,' said Mary Parkes. 'None of them are – I mean is – being taught any more.'

'You be – I mean will be – teacher.'

'Impossible.'

'Where there's a way, there's a will. You good teacher. You teached me.'

'Taught.'

'Too right. You teach again. I come to school with all my kids. You know my kids. Me. Marriage.'

Mary Parkes took the box of lipsticks back to the refrigerator. 'I would have thought that with all your kids you knew all you need to know about marriage. Anyway, your husband-to-be, who is he?'

'More better, you don't know. He don't know.'

'He doesn't?'

Bel giggled. 'I don't know.'

'You're being silly.'

Bel went through the doorway. 'Silly? When I know, he know. When he know, I know. When we know, you know.'

16

Ogilvie held the coffin at arm's length, slid it onto the girders above his bed and stepped back to inspect his corner of the Bachelor Quarters.

Something wrong. His boots. He stooped to examine them and a slice of stale bread hit him on the back of the head.

He straightened, swung round and then crouched. For a first-pressure, split second, Sheean by the table and silhouetted black against the harsh, sunlit entrance to the Bachelor Quarters had been a pop-up target on a small-arms range, a pop-up target which now said, 'G'day mate. Missed your resurrection in the desert, did I?'

Ogilvie picked up the slice of stale bread. 'As well you did, Vin. Or I'd've planted you then and there.' He began to eat the bread as he walked towards the table where flies dog-fought over scraps of bacon, congealing egg and empty fruit tins while a two-way column of ants made off with grains of sugar and bread crumbs.

Sheean said, 'That's it, mate. Hop into the bread. There's no blood today.' He picked up a bottle from the table. 'Only tomato ketchup.'

Ogilvie bent down to examine one of the rusty fruit tins in which the table legs were set. 'You've let the tins go dry. Bloody ants are getting everything.'

Sheean broke a slice of bread precisely between his fingers, dipped the pieces in the tomato ketchup and scattered them on the table.

Feed my ants, he thought and said, 'They deserve it. They work harder than we do.'

Ogilvie gathered up the fragments and began eating them. 'Speak for yourself, your laziness, and get this place cleaned up.'

Sheean fingered the money in his pocket. Your thiefiness. Definitely time for him to be moving. 'I've got better things to do,' he said.

Ogilvie said, 'Listen, Vin. I don't think you realise how daft it is to think other people are as daft as you are.'

'Don't bother to try spelling that out, mate. I haven't got time.'

'You might have if ... Ach, for a man who says he's on the run from one woman, you're awful fond of chasing others.'

53

'Chase? I don't have to chase them. Know what Bel said to me this morning. She said –'

'Save it for a party piece. I want this whole bloody barracks cleaned up.'

'What? And spoil the contrast with your corner of this old bush shack that is for ever Aldershot?' Sheean pointed to the metal bed in the far corner of the long, corrugated-iron barracks.

Unlike the five other beds which were a rumple of sweaty blankets or bare mattresses, Ogilvie's bed was neatly made up, grey blankets squared off with mathematical exactitude.

Sheean flopped onto the bare mattress of his own bed. 'You're too fussy, mate. You need a woman to take your mind off the fatigues. Bel. She's as ready as the battery. And I don't mind sharing. Not with you. My word, I don't.'

'Your word's not worth its spit when you talk that way, Vin.' Ogilvie took a tin jug of water from the fridge and a tin of powdered milk. 'Who the hell do you think you're kidding?'

He tried to close the fridge. Sheean watched from his bed, amused. 'All right, mate. So it's been a long time and you've forgotten how. Bel knows enough for two.'

Sheean laughed. Ogilvie kick-slammed the fridge and roared, 'Shut your filthy gob, Vin. Or I'll fill it full of knuckles, so I will.'

Sheean laughed again. 'Wish you'd fill it as full of beer as you were last night. And whisky. I reckon you had more embalming fluid in you than King Tut when we put you in the coffin.'

Ogilvie spooned dried milk into a tea-stained enamel mug. He added water and a pinch of salt from a heap on the table. He stirred the mixture. The billy-goat bell clanked as the mob of goats came to drink at the trough outside the Bachelor Quarters. Sheean said, 'Have some of the tit fresh. Mary Parkes won't mind. She's only got one but she's generous with it.'

The enamel mug clanked against the corrugated iron wall above

Sheean's head. The milk in it spilled over him. Wash me in reconstituted milk, he thought, licking the milk running down his face. He wiped his face on his sleeve. And cleanse me.

'I'll have some of the tit fresh myself,' he said. 'Go on, mate. There's one begging to be milked.'

Ogilvie jinked left to tip the mattress and Sheean onto the floor and right to catch a bleating nanny with a full udder. 'This one had a kid,' he said.

Sheean crawled from under the mattress as Ogilvie drank off the water in the tin jug. When he began to milk the nanny into the jug, Sheean squatted beside him. 'I don't have to tell you who got the kid,' he said. 'Your faithful friend, Dustbin.'

The milk went ringing into the tin jug. Ogilvie said, 'More likely it was a dingo.'

'Dingo, my athlete's foot. It was Dustbin.'

'She's running with a dingo. It would have been him.'

'Her. The bold bitch, Dustbin.'

'Him. Him. The dingo.'

'Dustbin.' Sheean took a gold-coloured cigarette packet from the top pocket of his overalls and lit up. Ogilvie slapped the nanny on the rump and she clattered off to join the rest of the mob. He took a sup of the fresh milk. 'OK. OK. I've set a trap for her.'

Sheean lit up. 'Trap. It's a bullet she needs.'

'You're a bit of an urger, Vin. You shoot her if you're all that keen.'

'Lend me your rifle and it's done.' Sheean heaved the mattress back on his bed and lay down again.

Above Sheean's head was another coffin. No doubt about it. The Outback was a great school. In all the years he should've learnt, he hadn't noticed that coffin-makers didn't bother to French-polish the bottom of coffins. It wasn't until he'd started as a general labourer, spine-basher and grave digger with Magwu Shire Council that he'd learnt.

55

He winked at the pin-up winking at him from where she had been pasted on the bottom of the coffin. Bare bottom to bare bottom. Better than dust to dust. He blew a smoke ring towards her. It floated upwards and broke before it reached her head.

One day he would get a halo on her. St Pulchrituda of Porno, martyred to make a wanker's holiday by having a staple thrust through her belly button. Wanker. Bel had called him that.

He turned on his elbow and gazed at Matilda, his housekeeper. Maybe he should stick with her. She might be only an old dress-maker's dummy rescued from the older ruins of the pioneer home-stead on the farthest edge of town. Interesting woman, the pioneer wife, leaving behind Matilda, a side-saddle and the works of Marie Stopes. Sheean sat up at a thought. What if there hadn't been a woman? What if the pioneer'd laid out good money on a dress-maker's dummy, a side-saddle and the works of Marie Stopes for a woman who never came? Was that Australia? A woman who never came.

Anyway, Matilda was the perfect housekeeper. She didn't speak back and she reflected only as much of himself as he wanted to see.

Ogilvie held out the jug of milk. Sheean shook his head. Ogilvie put the jug of milk in the fridge. He went to Matilda and examined his face in the bathroom shelf fitment Sheean had fixed onto the dummy's neck.

Sheean said, 'If you're going to perv on Matilda, my house-keeper, you may as well take my Bel.'

'Bel's not yours.' Ogilvie picked up a tin mug from the shelf above his bed and went to the standpipe outside the door of the Bachelor Quarters. He turned on the tap. Water snorted out, hot from 4000 feet down.

'Hell's sweat,' said Ogilvie, stepping away from the overflow and filling his tin mug.

Sheean lay back again to try to fit a halo on St Pulchrituda of

56

Porno. He said to Ogilvie, 'You don't have to stay here on the hot backside of nowhere.' He puffed a smoke ring upwards. 'Like a flea between the cheeks of a Kalgoorlie tart.'

Ogilvie got a shaving brush, soap and a cut-throat razor from the shelf above his bed. He went back to Matilda, laid his gear out on the shelf fitment and began to lather up. 'What about yourself, Vin?'

'The old woman, mate. You know that. She's Scarlet by name and scarlet by nature. Not like Matilda who's sober, steadfast and demure. The old woman chases me all over the place. Her rights. She can smell me upwind, downwind, north, south, east and west. Everywhere. Sooner or later, there's a reminder.'

'Give it a rest, Vin.'

'A rest. I wish I could. I wish she would. And you. When I got myself jailed for using insulting language to get a rest after fixing you up with a berth back to Pommieland, who walked into the jail after me? You did, you big, no-hoper bastard.'

The cut-throat razor hung in the air. 'You're still not bad with the insulting language,' Ogilvie said.

Sheean coughed on a smoke ring. 'Sorry,' he said. 'Sorry, mate.'

The cut-throat razor rasped down Ogilvie's cheek. 'Forget it,' said Ovilgie. 'It was the rum that did for me. It's hard to judge the rum.'

Sheean said nothing. Only watched the razor seeming to carve the hard, tanned planes of Ogilvie's face from the soft, white lather.

Ogilvie wiped his cut-throat razor on the shoulder of the dressmaker's dummy. It wasn't just the rum. He'd wanted to get into the jail to tell Vin that he knew what Vin really was and to tell Vin what he himself'd done. He scraped another swathe of soap from his cheek.

'The screws, Vin,' he said, 'I couldn't've left you on your tod. The screws would've made mincemeat of you.'

Sheean leant out of bed and butted his cigarette on the concrete

57

floor. 'You were supposed to be on your way home. Back to the welfare womb.'

'You don't know what you're talking about.'

'Course I do. You Poms can't take life straight.'

'I'm no Pom, you Aussie –' Ogilvie broke off. He couldn't use the word bastard to Vin, to anyone.

'McPom then,' said Sheean. 'But you still can't take life straight. Heard about a Pom once who got a woman on the National Health Service. Oedipal Pom, he was. Got himself a nice sort of Jocasta on the National Health Service. Often wondered how it worked out. I mean he must've wanted a happy ending. Wouldn't happen to know him, would you?'

Ogilvie scraped round his chin. Sheean coughed. 'Maybe you could do with a happy ending, mate,' he said. 'Like Bel.'

'Aye, and maybe you know about a better happy ending, Vin?'

'Than Bel. Not in Rainbow. Not for you, mate. You were crying drunk again before you collapsed last night. Know that?'

The cut-throat razor sliced slivers of sunlight from the dusty air as Ogilvie whirled. 'Again? Again? What do you mean, again? I'll drink every Aussie in this country under the table. Crying drunk? Me?'

'Don't worry,' said Sheean, his eye on the razor. 'It was the grog. The grog crying. The grog talking.'

'Talking about what?'

'Nothing coherent.'

'Nothing about a bloke?'

'Nothing, I said. All you did was your usual. Funerals and the drill. Slow marching. Reversing arms. But no worries. We all have our mad moments up here and I can keep a secret. My oath, I can.'

'Vin, you weren't born to be a liar. Did I say anything about this bloke – ?'

'Nothing. I told you, it was your usual.'

'Vin, I've got to tell you about this bloke.'

58

'Shut up. Shut up. You told me last night about him. Your colonel-in-chief. Said you loved him.'

'Her.'

Sheean sat up in bed, laughing. 'Your colonel-in-chief was a woman?'

'A princess.'

'Oh,' said Sheean, and laughed again. 'I thought, colonel-in-chief, I thought maybe you loved him like a father. Now you tell me your colonel-in-chief was a woman, a princess.'

'Vin –'

'Don't worry, mate. I told you I can keep a secret. My oath I can.' He laughed again. 'Even the secret of your dear and only love.' Sheean got off his bed and walked towards the door. No way he was going to encourage any more of Ogilvie's secrets. He had listened to too many people who kept the worst to the last. Ogilvie going on about being an orphan brought up in a military school was bad enough. Hearing his colonel-in-chief was a princess – his dear and only love – was worse. This bloke must be Og's last and worst.

Sheean turned in the doorway. 'Let's have a drink,' he said.

Ogilivie tilted the mirror so that it caught Sheean's face: eyebrows clown-black against a round pallor. Aye, Ogilvie thought, you can keep every secret except your own.

'Vin,' he said again and cleaned the last of the soap from his own face and replaced the towel on the shoulder of the dressmaker's dummy. 'Vin . . .' But he couldn't tell Vin yet – any more than he could tell him in jail; any more than he could go back home and tell them on the barracks square. But he would somehow. He picked up a broom and lanced it at Sheean. 'Sweep it out, Vin. Sweep out the whole place.'

Sheean caught the broom and sat on the floor, gripping the broom handle crosswise in front of his knees with both hands. 'Pull you for it,' Og,' he said. 'You pull me, I do it. I pull you, you do it.'

59

Ogilvie poured water from his shaving mug into each of the cans which held the legs of the table.

Sheean said, 'Come on, you know what you say yourself when you're pissed.' And recited all in a rush, 'He either fears his fate too much/Or his deserts are small/That puts it not into the touch/To win or lose it all.'

Ogilvie sat down facing Sheean. His hands gripped the broom handle on the outside of Sheean's who started to pull immediately. Ogilvie pulled in the opposite direction. Sheean held. Ogilvie put his full strength into his effort. Sheean let go. Ogilvie went over backwards. Sheean laughed as Ovilgie turned his fall into a back flip, regaining his feet with the broom still gripped in his hands.

Sheean applauded. He knew he should stop teasing Og. But the risk was irresistible. 'What a talent,' he said. 'Absolutely blinding.'

'Unlike you,' said Ogilvie.

He began to sweep out the Bachelor Quarters, sending the dust flying towards the door and the desert.

'Streuth,' said Sheean, 'I should've put a label round your neck when I farewelled you that time. You would've been there by now and not here annoying me.'

Ogilvie dropped the broom. 'Finish it.'

'Finish it yourself, McPom.'

'Finish it, Vin. Or I'll finish you.'

Sheean clasped the dressmaker's dummy. 'Oh, save me, Mother. Save me from the mad McPom who loves the colonel-in-chief.'

Ogilvie went outside, across the flat to where Rainbow's water tank stood high on a cross-braced steel scaffold. Sheean followed, waltzing the dressmaker's dummy and singing, 'Oh, save me, Mother. Save me from the mad McPom who loves the colonel-in-chief, the princess.'

With a roar that was more pain than rage, Ogilvie grabbed the dressmaker's dummy and heaved it through the air. It landed on the mirror which shattered and snapped off at the handle.

'Seven years bad luck for a broken mirror,' said Sheean.

'How many for a broken promise, Vin?'

Ogilvie turned to the water tank. Polythene pipes ran from a row of stopcock valves attached to the tank's main outlet. The valves were tagged. 'School', 'Ablutions', 'Pub', and 'Bachelor Quarters'. A vacant valve was tagged 'Church'. Ogilvie coupled this valve to the end of a polythene pipe which snaked off under the sand.

'Definitely, the mad McPom,' said Sheean when Ogilvie opened the stopcock, 'I'll lay you odds, the tap's on at the other end and the water's gushing everywhere.'

'No bet,' said Ogilvie, 'I know the tap's on.'

'Dill,' said Sheean. 'Water's precious up here.'

'It's no good without people.'

'You've got everything worked out then.'

Ogilvie stood up and stared at Sheean. 'Everything,' he said. 'Including you, mate.'

17

Bobbie Maley and all Bel's other kids danced round the tap from which water was pouring. Their dogs joined them. Bobbie put his finger on the tap, spraying water on the kids and dogs who danced more wildly, shrieking and barking in delight.

The noise brought Bel out of the corrugated iron shack Ogilvie had thatched with brushwood. Bobbie went to her and Harold took over spraying the kids and dogs.

'Good camp, Mum, eh?' Bobbie shouted.

'Good camp, Mum. Good camp, Mum. Good camp, Mum,' the kids chorused.

Bel's smile took in the four shacks, the concrete raft, the running

61

water, the kids and Bobbie. 'More better than where we are, son. More better than those government fellas made it,' she said. 'Turn off our water. We bin moving here.'

Harold wouldn't turn off the tap until Bobbie cuffed him. The kids cheered and Harold led the rush to the old humpies to collect their bedding.

Bel and Bobbie went into the brushwood-thatched shack to work out which kids should go where.

'That Harold,' said Bobbie.

'That Harold's your brother,' said Bel, and ticked off the names of the kids. 'Cooler here for them,' she added.

'Yeah,' said Bobbie. 'Maybe you got the wrong bloke, Mum. That Vin, he's a bit of a no-hoper.'

'Maybe,' said Bel and went to the door. Bobbie moved alongside her and she put her arm round his shoulders.

They drew in a breath together. Boondoo was riding down the track towards them on Lubra. Behind him streamed kids and dogs. Alongside trotted Olga, carrying his didjeridu. Boondoo himself controlled Lubra one-handed. In his other hand, he carried a smouldering branch – fire for the new camp.

18

Throwing up a bow wave of red dust, Donaldson drove his prime-mover and trailers towards another blue mirage. His roaring prime-mover swallowed the mirage. And then Donaldson felt that the mirage in turn had swallowed him and changed him. He was in his best clobber, gold-threaded cowboy shirt, feather Akubra hat, blue jeans, big buckle belt and high-heeled R. M. Williams boots when he heard a Pom with a plummy accent mention the name Donaldson hated.

'Yes,' the Pom added to the great chick who was with him, 'I'm chairman of the board, don't you know? What's more, my dear, we had a record profit this year.'

Donaldson swung the Pom round and smashed his fist into his teeth. He knew the Pom was made of too many pills and too much piss. But his hatred of the Pom was real.

'Cop that for twenty-six per cent true rate on truck finance, you bludging bastard,' Donaldson yelled.

The Pom went down, flatter than steamrollered. Donaldson saw the chick lift the blond curtain of her hair from one eye and it was mirage blue. Donaldson knew that the chick was also made of too many pills and too much piss. But he loved the way she said, 'I've been hoping you would do that before the little Pommie drongo bored me to death. Your place or mine?'

'Yours,' said Donaldson. 'I'll supply the truck.'

'Did you say truck?' asked the chick.

Her laughing mouth was like the inside of a watermelon.

'Shit,' said Donaldson as he turned the juddering wheel of his prime-mover hard left to pass the white four-wheel drive which came hurtling towards him out of the chick's laughing, red mouth.

A cloud shuddering blood. And before Tim Webster at the wheel of the four-wheel drive realised that the cloud was a mangled sheep flying from the jack-knifed road-train, Tembo Halliday was out of the vehicle and shooting.

'Oath,' said Webster, switching off the ignition and letting the story start in his mind. A sheep. Tembo Halliday shot a flying sheep. A story for the pubs and the years . . . Wouldn't've believed it if I hadn't seen it with me own eyes. On the Rainbow Track, it was. A road-train going down like the Devil on skates. And me with me foot on the accelerator coming up. Don't know how I stopped in time. Don't know how the road-train driver did. Anyway, jack-knifed and this jumbuck went flying. Like a bloody cloud, it was.

Scores of sheep, baaing crazily were spilling out of the road-train. And Halliday was levering round after round of his pain into them.

Webster got out of the four-wheel drive and ran to where Donaldson lay. Kiss of life, thought Webster as he bent over Donaldson who groaned and heaved himself into a sitting position. Webster shouted, 'Mongrel bastard, I'll fucking kiss of life you. Hell're you doing on this track with sheep? Sheep! Hell're you doing?'

Donaldson touched his head and looked at the blood on his hand.

'Giving me dandruff a transfusion,' he said.

Halliday's rifle cracked again and again. Donaldson noticed it for the first time.

'Who's your mad mate?' he said.

'Tembo Halliday.'

'The Yank writer?'

Webster nodded and Donaldson went on, 'Read one of his books once. Wasn't as good as the cover. You sure he's all right?' Donaldson stood up, holding his head carefully as if he thought it might roll off his neck. 'Tell him to save the last round for me. Of all the mugs. Of all the dillpot mugs.'

Webster picked up Donaldson's hat and handed it to him. 'You still haven't told me what you were doing on this track with sheep.'

'Trying to pay for my plant.'

'With sheep? They're not worth a cracker.'

Donaldson eased his hat on. 'Not to you maybe. But there's more to sheep than prices. Let me give you the drum.'

And he did while Halliday shot his rifle hotter and sheep died like men, their eyes glistening in the sun, jewels for the kitehawks circling.

When Donaldson finished explaining, Webster laughed. 'I've

heard of blokes making a quid in some ways up here. But you. You beat them all. My oath, you do.'

Donaldson was silent, staring at Sue Cornwall. Spitting image of the chick with the Pom. But not made of too many pills and too much piss. Sugar and spice. And as real as a ride. But just like the chick he had imagined. Tall enough to challenge a man. Yeah, just like the chick. Except for the red hair. And the freckles. How far did they go? How far would she?

Donaldson moved towards her, swayed, recovered and headed towards the road-train. Halliday reloaded his rifle and began to fire into the scrambled mob of sheep again.

Shit and derision. Could this be the cure? Transferring his pain to these sheep down the hot barrel of his rifle?

He brought the crosshairs of his telescopic sight to bear on a tup which was clattering away from the wreckage. Pain pincered him. The crosshairs wavered.

He needed more than sheep. He needed a big rhino. Or better, a simba, a lion coming at him with a disembowelling roar. That was the cure. He would've been taking the cure, too, had it not been for Jitu, the Giant, self-styled, who'd swapped his brolly for a flywhisk to return from the pissant London School of Economics as father of his country. Jitu, that black son of a bitch, had shafted him. Double shafted him. Shafted him in black Africa and what was left of white. *Persona non grata* wherever the game herds still ran and the lion and the leopard still hunted them. The other black leaders didn't much care how many times Tembo Halliday had bedded one of Jitu's women. Laughed, even, at the Giant Who Holds Up the Sun being cuckolded. But they stopped laughing when Jitu put it about that Tembo Halliday was a spy for the South African government and then tipped of the South Africans that Tembo Halliday had been recruited as a Jitu agent in a black woman's bed.

Oh cunning Jitu. He knew how to shut a hunter out of the last paradise. The crosshairs steadied. The rifle cracked. The tup dropped. Four hundred yards at least. And going away.

Halliday caught a movement to his left. He swung to find himself sighting on Ashby, whose camera was fixed to his eye.

'Ought to get transplant, Fisi. Camera instead of your eye,' Halliday shouted.

No doubt about it. Ashby did look like a hyena, trained hyena, his head bowed between his shoulders from tearing at the guts of the dead.

And the dying.

Halliday fired. Ashby held his ground as the shot dropped a sheep near him. 'Yeah, camera big juju,' Halliday said.

By the road-train with Webster, Donaldson laughed. Webster patted him on the shoulder. 'Easy, mate. She'll be all right.'

Donaldson shrugged his hand off. 'Don't worry about me. I'm going to show those bludgers Down Below a trick that'll cost them as much as I've been sweating.'

He picked up the swag he had retrieved from the road-train cabin and carried it across to the four-wheel drive where he stowed it on the roof rack among the other luggage. He went back to the road-train and unstrapped his water bags from the front bull bar. Halliday said to Webster. 'He planning to leave his rig here?'

Donaldson said, ''S not mine, mate.'

Halliday said, 'We can call up help on our radio. Breakdown crew.'

Donaldson and Webster looked at each other. Donaldson said, 'Not my worry.' He took a drink from one of the water bags. 'Thirsty work.' He held the water bag out to Halliday. 'Butchering.'

Halliday shook his head, 'Got to see to the rest of them first.'

Donaldson said, 'You've given the kitehawks a bit of a feed. I

66

reckon the coons deserve the the rest. They'll be easier to kill than roos.'

Out on the flat, the sheep were bunching together and heading towards water. The kitehawks were already quarrelling over the eyes of dead sheep.

Halliday aimed his rifle and fired a shot which sent the kitehawks soaring. 'Concubines.'

'Say again,' said Donaldson.

'In a harem. Those birds. Reminded me of goddamn concubines in a harem fattening themselves up to be fucked by an oil sheik sick of skinny lays in London.'

'Rave on,' said Donaldson and carried his water bags to the four-wheel drive. Halliday turned to Webster. 'That guy sounds crazy to me. Concussed maybe.'

Webster stared at Halliday. So what's the matter with you? he wondered. Yabbering on about the kitehawks and concubines, an oil sheik and skinny lays. And shouting 'Shit and derision'. What kind of a way was that for a man to talk?

'Shit and derision,' said Halliday. 'Concussed. I'm sure of it.'

'All I know is what he told me,' said Webster. 'He's been running jumbucks that aren't worth a cracker up north to the markets Down Below for a bloke who's getting a five-dollar drought grant from the government for every head delivered.'

'Shit and derision,' said Halliday. 'That beats both ends against the middle. So why does he want to leave his rig out here?'

'He's going to hit someone with it,' said Webster. 'Hard. Bloody oath. And where it hurts most.'

'"Bloody oath"?' said Halliday. 'That's a good one. Shit and derision it is. If my second wife wasn't citing "Shit and derision" as evidence of verbal cruelty, I would switch to "Bloody oath" – shit and derision I would.'

'A man has to be able to say something,' said Webster. 'Otherwise what's the point of hitting your bloody thumb with the bloody hammer.'

'Yeah. But it's a helluva note when your wife's lawyers call you on your language while arguing she should get a share of your royalties.'

'Wouldn't know about that, Tembo. Maybe you should just give her rights to "Shit and derision".'

Halliday guffawed. 'Might just do that small thing, Tim. Shit and derision I might.'

Webster moved towards the four-wheel drive. Sometimes talking to clients was harder yakka than singing to cows.

19

Des Parkes finished carving the last letter of his Grandpa Jim's full name and stepped back to admire his work. The old name board from the *River Queen* had hardened with the years. It had taken him longer than he expected to carve on it, 'This vessel won at cards by James Reilly Parkes'.

One day, he would have to gild the addendum to match 'River Queen'. He lifted the name board and hooked it back on the chains which held it suspended behind the saloon bar. Yeah, definitely a mighty man, Grandpa Jim.

Des Parkes turned at the sound of footsteps. Ogilvie and Sheean. Trouble and more trouble. For a moment, Des Parkes wished that the mighty man were with him to act as bouncer. Sheean, barefooted, was carrying a pair of carpet slippers. In the toe of each was a can of beer.

'G'day, Des,' he said. 'You look like I feel.'

'So why don't you give us both a rest?'

Sheean thumped the cans on the counter. 'Coldies for these.'

'The No Grog flag's flying.'

'Come on, Des. Everyone knows you've got a party coming through from Down Below. But regulars first, eh?'

Des Parkes took the two cans, turned to a cold cupboard, put them in and took out two cold cans. 'Last two,' he said.

Sheean's can went in a rip and a couple of long swallows. He put his hand on his heart, smiling. 'It's started again. But it's still a bit unsure of itself. Same again.'

'I said those were the last two.'

'The two I gave you weren't all that warm. They'll be cold enough by the time you get them out.'

'Money,' said Des Parkes.

'Next payday.'

'No way.'

Sheean turned to Ogilvie, 'Your shout, mate.'

Ogilvie raised his can. 'Plenty of time.' He took a swallow of beer. Of all the daft remarks. Especially after his dream. That had made him think time had run out on him. As it would.

'Look,' said Des Parkes, 'I'm not carrying you for another dollar. You're into me for fifty-two already.'

Sheean turned and threw the empty beer can out the door onto the flat. 'You've got his rifle as security.'

'His rifle's no bloody good unless he's using it and I'm not giving it back until the pair of you cough up what you owe. With interest.'

'Break it down, Des,' said Sheean. 'You'll have your granddad haunting you.'

'Get out. Out. I don't want to see your stinking, boozy face in my pub again.'

Des Parkes helped himself to a quick rum. Trouble about being descended from a legend was everybody knew how his grandpa always said what was wrong with Australia was it treated the original owners the way it should treat its bloody bankers.

Des Parkes gave himself another rum. Bastard Sheean. Duff of a face. Currant eyes. Bastard. Looked as if he'd crawled out the cooking pot before he was done.

'Out,' said Des Parkes. He washed the rum glass and put it on the draining board. Sheean began to collect empty glasses from around the saloon bar.

'Leave those bloody glasses alone,' Des Parkes shouted. 'I don't want you in my pub. You frightened my wife last night. That bloody coffin. She really thought someone was really a goner.'

Sheean put a clutch of dirty glasses on the counter. 'I'll apologise.'

'Keep away from her, you combo bastard. Don't think I didn't see you climbing out of Bel's cot.'

'Envy, Des, envy,' said Sheean. 'You've got to watch the green eye – especially the green eye about another bloke's sins. Coveting thy neighbour's wife is bad enough but coveting his adultery –'

'That black bitch. She's as ugly as a hatful of backsides. I wouldn't touch her with a ten-foot pole.'

'It wasn't a ten-foot pole you tried to touch her with as I heard it. Four inches full out.'

'I never touched her.'

'You couldn't catch her.'

'Out, you –'

A whistle interrupted Des Parkes. He picked up a speaking tube behind the bar. 'Yes, darl,' he said and put the tube to his ear, turning his head away as if Sheean and Ogilvie could hear. 'Yes, darl. Yes, darl.'

Sheean laughed. Parkes bent down and took a rifle from beneath the bar. He held it out to Ogilvie. 'Your dog has got Mary worried. Apparently one of her goats is missing. She wants you to do something about it.'

Ogilvie worked the bolt of the rifle. 'Can't do anything without another couple of beers. And the rest of my gear.'

Parkes put three ammunition clips on the counter and a webbing belt with bayonet attached. Ogilvie snapped the belt on as Des Parkes turned to the cold cupboard to get the beers.

20

Tembo Halliday bent forward until his chin was resting on the muzzle of the rifle held between his knees. Still the thing, the creature swam in the rising tide of pain towards his brain. His finger found the safety catch. His thumb moved to the trigger. The four-wheel drive jolted in and out of a pothole.

Shit and derision. The fear. The explosive fear of thinking for a split second that the jolt would blow his head off. The fear as the thing, the creature created from him, fled on the ebbing tide of pain.

Halliday raised his head. How many years was he looking at? Not as many as the miles he could see.

What this country needed was lion. Yeah, and kudu, impala, gazelle and zebra. That guy in Texas had the right idea, stocking his acres with game against the time when Jitu and his buddies decided the Limey groundnuts scheme wasn't a big enough disaster and put game plains under the plough as so much of the world had been.

Old bank clerk Tom Eliot had it right. The world would end with a whimper. Not a bang. The whimper of the wind blowing the world's topsoil into the sea.

The four-wheel drive roared forward into Halliday's past. Fisi had been needling him, asking Tim Webster about North Africa in 1941 and '42.

Fisi was a tombstone. Had all the dates. Knew '41 was year Halliday's Irregulars were recruited. And not in North Africa. South. Twenty-twenty hindsight, Fisi – thought it funny Halliday's Irregulars should've been recruited to stop Kraut landing to

71

pillage southwest diamond fields. Yet everyone knew Hitler was mad enough to try anything. Fisi knew. Knew experts all said Halliday's Irregulars were worth a battalion before he disbanded them to get to Italy.

Halliday turned in his seat, shouting, 'Goddamn tombstone, you knew, Fisi, you knew.' Ashby raised one of his cameras and clicked off a shot. 'Dust jacket specimen, Tembo,' he said.

Tim Webster was fighting the gears to bring the four-wheel drive out of a wave of sand. Halliday said, 'Seen better roads in Africa. Matter of fact, it isn't a road. Coincidence of ruts looking for a destination. Right, Bibi?'

Sue Cornwall moved away from his hand. The four-wheel drive slewed as Tim Webster moved away from her. Jeez, if a man had known there was going to be a sheila along and that Tembo Halliday was going to be riding her in public.

'Whether woman makes great mistress or great wife,' said Halliday, 'depends on who gets to her first.'

Sue Cornwall said, 'Tape that, Ashby.'

'Forget him, Bibi. He's got nothing for you. But whoever got to you first – boy, do the travel agents owe him a commission.'

'Piss off. I can't stand men who are under the impression women belong to the first man who breaks and enters them.'

'Hear that, Tim?' said Halliday.

Webster sounded the horn by way of reply. Jeez, what was an old gin burglar supposed to say? This sheila was a hard sort. A cold, hard sort. And her voice. A man didn't realise how soft a gin's voice was till he heard a white sheila shrieking the silence into tintacks.

'Don't, don't,' she was shrieking. 'Don't.'

Webster sounded the horn again, a long blast, and Halliday said, 'Cool it, Bibi. Cool it. Not your fault you didn't make it big like your friend what's-her-name?'

Sue Cornwall was silent. What's-her-name? Nelly Carpenter,

72

Australia's top model and sole proprietor of the Starway Modelling Academy (branches in all capitals) whose curriculum included lessons in the use of the fork and knife. Nelly had never needed a lesson. Her tongue was both her fork and her knife. 'Lovely, lovely, lazy Suzie. Lovely to see you, lovely. But you're still not really working at your modelling, are you?'

Nelly, swimming in her own tide of scent, her capped teeth too big for her fined-down face. Nelly with so much gloop on her face you felt that under all the layers, her skull would be rusty.

Of all the places to see her: Canberra, where Halliday reckoned the trees outnumbered the bureaucrats but were less dense. Nelly'd gone to freshen up, and a blur trying to define himself by familiarity with power figures said, 'Would you believe, your friend's husband is only a back-stabbing away from the prime-ministership?' It took a second for it to become clear that the blur was talking about Nelly's husband. It took another second to realise who Nelly's husband was.

Nelly returned with a new layer of gloop, two brimming glasses of orange juice and champagne. 'I've heard Tembo Halliday prefers older women, duckie. You don't qualify,' she said. 'This year.' Her spiky, black eyelashes had blinked. 'Come over and talk to Glenn. He'll be delighted to see you again after all this time.'

Luckily, Halliday had gone over the top just then about the number of ex-newspapermen in attendance on the politicians.

'Shit and derision,' he'd shouted. 'Every other guy here's carrying a big bucket of red herrings. Newspapermen I worked with would sooner have kissed Al Capone's syphilitic ass than signed on as a politician's red-herring-bucket carrier. What is this anyway – a finks' convention?'

He had swayed towards the Prime Minister who'd given his famous imitation of an Easter Island statue when Halliday put his arm round his shoulders for the benefit of a passing photographer.

73

Now Halliday's arm was round her shoulders as the four-wheel drive headed north and west, chewing distance and spitting dust.

Australia was all distance. Men trying to swim to each other through oceans of grog. Women throwing out nets of gossip to catch a friend.

And Glenn, solving the country's big problems in multilateral association with other politicians. Pity he couldn't've taken one of his positive initiatives when she was pregnant with their little problem whose name she would never know, only the vacant despair of his death. Funny that, she had always known it was a boy.

21

Ogilvie led off, his rifle at the trail, his boots crunching out a light infantry pace on the track which twisted through fire-blackened scrub and rock towards the gorge. Behind him, Sheean scattered more brightly wrapped lollies, like butterflies, to persuade the kids who were following that this was not the time for a swim.

Gradually the kids fell back as the lollies took hold till only Bobbie Maley was left.

'Oh, all right, you little bastard,' said Sheean, 'keep stunting your growth,' and threw him a cigarette.

Bobbie Maley halted then and took out a cigarette lighter. Ogilvie saw him. 'Smoke that and I'll warm your backside for you,' he roared.

Bobbie Maley lit the cigareette and fled, puffing. Ogilvie switched his anger to Sheean.

'You shouldn't give that kid cigarettes. Any kid.'

Sheean laughed. 'Terrific. The perfect solution. I'll keep Bel happy in bed. You can be father to her kids.'

Ogilvie did not reply but set off again at the double. A man could do worse than inherit a family, sons, daughters. Bel. She was going to need someone.

Sheean in his carpet slippers put on a spurt and managed to pass Ogilvie, clinking. Ogilvie increased his pace and regained the lead, shouting, 'Keep that money quiet. You sound like a piggy bank running away to paint the town red.'

Sheean thrust the roll of notes deeper into his pocket to silence the loose change. 'I need a rest.'

'We've only this minute started.'

'That's what I mean, you dill, a rest before we really start. Anyway we should wait for Boondoo. We need a tracker.'

'To catch my own dog? Don't be daft.'

Their way ran parallel to the river where it flowed from the gorge. Sheean halted. The dry had cut the river into a string of pools linked by strands of sand, patterned with roo trails. Sheean shouted, 'What's that? There over behind the ghost gum. Swear it was your dog.'

Ogilvie unloaded the rifle and leant it against a tree. 'If it's a rest you want and a cup of char, say so.'

'Oath.'

'Then leave your specs and go and fill the billycan.'

Sheean took his specs from his pocket, gave them to Ogilvie and walked to the nearest pool. Ogilvie gathered together a heap of dead gum leaves, walling them in with stones and sand. He focused the sun on a gum leaf, using Sheean's specs.

In the pool, Sheean, carpet slippers and all, sank in the sand. For a second, he felt weightless. He dipped the billycan in the pool. The brown water went silvery on the lip of the billycan. Off near the pub, a goat bell clanked in the Sunday silence. All he needed was a howling baby. Bel would give him that if he did not get away. She wanted another daughter. Pattie Menzies Maley. A close call this morning.

75

Bit of a puzzler about the poor bloody wanker Onan. Was it his wife who told? Women always talked about that kind of thing. If Eve had had any neighbours, everyone would know the true nature of the Fall.

Ogilvie shouted, 'Get a juldee on.'

The gum leaf was smoking. A black spot appeared on it. Then a red centre in the black spot and a tiny flame. Ogilvie added gum twigs, broken branches.

When Sheean returned with the billycan full of water, the fire was crackling, pale in the sun. Ogilvie jammed the billycan deep into the fire before giving the specs back.

Sheean said, 'You should carry matches.'

Ogilvie spat out a fly which had got into his mouth. 'Used my last match this morning. Anyway, you should wear the specs. Might stop you imagining you're seeing things.'

Sheean put the specs on and shaped up to Ogilvie, bobbing and weaving. 'Go on, try and hit me, you big Scots drongo. Go on, just try.' He whipped off the specs. 'And I'll turn into Super-bloody-man and smite you.' His left hand shot out. Ogilvie dodged the punch and said, 'See us the sugar and tea.' Sheean passed them over. The milky brown water in the billycan was bubbling. Ogilvie tipped the sugar and tea into the water and eased the billycan off the fire with his bayonet.

'Careful,' said Sheean.

'Nae bother.' Ogilvie began to swing the billycan from side to side. Steam rose from it. Sheean squinted up at the sun, blazing all gold at the edges and white as bread at its heart. He grinned. Hymn God. Me nothing but a punster wrapped inside a liar wrapped inside a tea leaf.

Ogilvie took a sup of tea. He held the billycan out to Sheean. A flock of galahs clattered pink against the big, blue sky.

'Five you don't hit one,' said Sheean, drinking.

76

'Couldn't, Vin. The galah's your totem bird.'

'Comedian. You've got to be, I suppose, with that accent and that funny hat.'

'How many times do I have to tell you? It's a Balmoral.'

'It's a hoot, mon. And you're definitely a comedian. A Presbo comedian, predestined to joke.'

'You don't know the half of it, Vin. And when you do, you'll realise there's no escaping what you are.'

'Exactly,' said Sheean, 'so stop trying to escape being a Presbo comedian in a funny hat predestined to joke. Un-bloody-believable.'

Ogilvie rubbed his forearm across his face, touching the bruise-like mark with his lips. It was un-bloody-believable. But no joke.

When he first joined the Regiment, one of the things that struck him was the hard-case RCs on church parade. Hung over. But bags of swank as they marched to Mass. He hadn't been too sure what Mass was then. Still, he shouldn't've been surprised later on in Palestine when the hardest of the hard cases, Rodd, moaned about getting to Mass. Shug Rodd. In the guardroom. Conduct preju-dicial. Rodd Hugh, Private, 861. Thumping an officer. Rodd in the guardroom, waiting to go to the glasshouse and a jacket that but-toned up the back if he thumped anyone else, moaning about getting to Mass. Midnight Mass. And what would he say to his old lady when she asked him about midnight Mass? Moaning, 'You've got to let me go, sarge. Here of all places. Come on, we were muckers. And you're regimental, not provost.'

Ogilvie stared at the bruiselike mark. Un-bloody-believable all right. Maybe that was why he'd come to believe it.

Three stripes lost because he couldn't refuse Rodd, his old mucker from whom the stripes had separated him. Three stripes. Maybe if he hadn't gone with Rodd to midnight Mass to make sure he came back. Maybe ... Ach, maybe nothing. It was a daft thing

77

to do and he would do it again if he could because it was the best thing as well.

Ogilvie poured the rest of the tea hissing on the fire.

Sheean laughed. 'You big dill. You didn't drink any of it.'

Ogilvie began heaping sand onto the smoking fire with his foot. 'You're not here to tell me I didn't drink my tea. You're not. You're here to . . .'

Silence stretched between them. Sheean headed for the gorge. To hell with tomorrow. Now was the acceptable time. Now was the day of running. He wasn't going to be around for Ogilvie's last and worst. He was building up to it. The orphan bit. The Army bit. The Jerusalem bit. The Ireland bit. And this bloke. A friend by the sound of it. Or a brother. But could that be in view of the orphan bit? Sheean felt in his pockets. What did it matter? He had the money. All he had to do was run.

Ogilvie made certain the fire was out. He'd missed another chance to tell Vin. He had to tell Vin. He had to. He reloaded his rifle and followed him, shouting, 'Here, Vin. Listen to me.'

Even as he shouted, Ogilvie knew he wasn't going to be able to tell Sheean. Not yet.

22

Vodka Mahonsky hated driving, especially the tractor. The noise of it blocked out the music of the wind in the wire. It did not prevent his hearing his mate, Sudan, standing beside him holding onto the post-hole drilling rig and shouting, 'Get a wriggle on, you reffo bastard. You're driving like a blind mouse looking for its tail in a fog.'

Mahonsky nodded and slowed down to study the fence which ran on the nearside of the track. One of his and Sudan's. Ten miles and still good for at least five more years. They needed another fencing contract. Not like the pub. Further in. A bush contract. Hundred miles, say. Piles of gidgee posts waiting to be set up. Reel upon reel of wire waiting to be strained for the wind to sing through.

'Get a wriggle on, I said,' Sudan yelled. 'The blokes in Rainbow'll be doing a perish.'

Vodka nodded, 'Your blame. You pranged the ute last night.'

'Bloody comical that.'

'I do not think so.'

'You reffo blow-ins are all the same. No sense of humour.'

Vodka glanced back to make sure the trailer loaded with beer was still hooked up to the tractor.

'Keep your eye on the track,' Sudan yelled, tugging at Vodka's ear. 'I'll keep my eye on the flaming beer.'

Vodka nodded and stared up at Sudan, old and lean and tougher than any gidgee posts. Comical, too. When they were bush on a contract, he didn't yell. He didn't talk at all. They were mates. They didn't need to talk. All they had to do was string the wire across the country, string it straight, string it tight, bringing wind music into the silence where they camped at night under the stars. Yet as soon as they finished a contract and came into town, Sudan started yelling. Something about these Aussies. Their noisy fronts hid fear. But then he also had been afraid. He was here. Not where he belonged, outlasting the poor, stupid Communists.

'Get a wriggle on, you reffo bastard. Hurry. Hurry.' Sudan took off his wide-brimmed hat and began to beat Vodka.

A man had to be mad to have a reffo mate. This one for sure. Head on him like a bloody boulder set on a bloody boulder. No way to hurt him. Hit him and you hit rock. Might as well hit him with . . . Sudan glared at the red rag fluttering from the end of one of the gidgee posts which stuck out over the end of the trailer.

79

Bloody reffo. Hit him with a gidgee post. Time was when a man could take his pick of dinkum Aussies for mates. Not now. All six feet under. Bloody reffo, Vodka Mahonsky. He could fence, though. Mad as a meat axe. But he could fence. Never a straighter line. Never a tighter wire.

Sudan put his hat back on. Christ, he was thinking like a fencer. Sudan O'Brien, the ringer, first to lead them and head them, a fencer with a reffo mate.

Still holding onto the post-hole drilling rig with his right hand, he inched across the tow bar towards the trailer and clambered into it. The ice packed round the beer was melting and dripping onto the track. Sudan took off his hat, put a chunk of ice in it and replaced his hat. Lovely. He turned over one of the beer cartons and opened the bottom to get at a can of beer. When he pulled the ring, the beer squirted and hissed into his open mouth. Lovely. Lovely.

'Want a beer, you old reffo bastard,' he shouted.

Mahonsky nodded. Sudan took another gulp of beer. 'Then come and get it. I'm not your bloody servant.'

Mahonsky slammed the brakes on the tractor. Sudan was jolted off his feet. 'Trying to kill me, you reffo bastard. Is that it? Want a real funeral, do you? Not like last night with old Og mollo in the coffin.'

He shook up the can of beer and squirted Mahonsky as he came towards the trailer.

Mahonsky roared, 'Enough, you bastard.'

'Who're you calling a bastard?' said Sudan. 'You reffo bastard. I'm Sudan Patrick Parnell O'Brien, named for a war, a saint and a politician, with papers to prove it. So where are yours?'

Mahonsky took a can of beer from the carton. 'I'm Vodka,' he said, opening the can, 'with beer chaser.'

It was an old exchange and they both laughed before drinking.

23

Ogilvie waited, crouched below the skyline, the wind in his face, the silence becoming so intense he could hear his heart beating, Sheean next to him breathing and again the rattle of the chain securing the dingo trap to its steel peg. Sheean nudged Ogilvie who shook his head.

He did not want to look. He was sure it was his dog, caught in the trap, trying to gnaw her way through the links of the chain.

Dustbin, Vin called her. He let him. But there was no way he could kill her any more than he could kill the memory of being ordered forward to take charge of the new mascot at the Institute. Mascot corporal. His first promotion. And him scarcely shoulder-high to the wolfhound, Bran.

Sheean motioned to him to pass the rifle. Ogilvie shook his head. Still crouching, he moved forward to the edge of the gorge. He eased the rifle to his shoulder. Only when he was ready to fire did he look down and across the gorge to where he had baited the trap.

Rear sight. Not her. Foresight. Not her. Both aligned. Not her. He held on the dingo's head where it was gnawing not at the chain but at its own leg above where it was caught by the steel teeth of the trap. He took first pressure and squeezed off the round on his own held breath.

'Missed,' said Sheean.

The impact of the .303 round jerked the dingo to the limit of the chain as it died. Ogilvie ejected the spent round and put another round up the spout. He picked up the spent case and put in the pocket of his shorts: a spent cartridge case on the ground may be found – and kill you.

McAskill lecturing on Deep Penetration Patrols: dos and don'ts. Schoolmaster voice. Killer eyes. And worse.

'Amazing,' said Sheean. 'The blokes in my mob always said a Pom couldn't hit a roo if he was sitting in its pouch.'

'Give it a by, Vin. I'm not in the mood for your tales today.'

'Just because I served with the best bloody mob in the world.'

'Aye, maybe. And maybe you should put your specs back on and go back to serving with that mob.'

Sheean slapped his paunch. 'Bit out of condition, compared to the way I was with the first and fittest in Korea, 1950.'

'I always thought the third Australians were first in there.'

'You know something?' said Sheean. 'You're right. I get mixed up. I got myself a transfer from the first to the third. They're both my mobs.'

'Ach, away with you, Vin. There's no transferring from your mob.'

Ogilvie handed Sheean the rifle, walked back fifteen paces, turned and ran for the edge of the gorge; ran, roaring 'Easy! Easy!' and leapt into the river.

His roar, long-drawn-out and echoing met him like a drill command of Sergeant Death's when he surfaced and breaststroked to where the dingo's carcase lay.

He took out his bayonet, jabbed its point into the dingo's muzzle and began to scalp it.

The best. They'd all said that. All the sergeants visiting the Institute to recruit for their regiments. Old sweats, solemn as schoolkids, reciting regimental histories as though they were scratched on the inside front of their skulls. Except the Scots Guards sergeant. He recited what was written on the inside of his cap vizor which came down over his nose.

Ogilvie sawed at the dingo, his hands bloody. He himself had been for the Guards. Right height. Right weight. Right eye with a rifle.

Until a tall, pale soldier came onto the square and introduced himself. 'I am Colour Sergeant De Ath. Colour Sergeant Alisdair De Ath of the Regiment which is acknowledged the greatest in the British Army. That is to say the world. Now then, you lads, you can call me Sergeant to my face for the time being and Sergeant Death behind my back for ever more.'

A tall, pale soldier in the dark green tunic of the Regiment and the tartan with the red line in it that he said went all the way back through Rome's Celtic levies to Calvary.

A tall, pale soldier talking about the Regiment and its long-ago battles as if they had happened yesterday and he had taken part in all of them. As if he had been with the Regiment on its way abroad when the troopship hit a rock.

Women and children first, with the sharks circling and the troopship sinking. Every last man in his rank, standing fast on the deck. 'Not a move, lads. Not a murmur.'

And the unbeatable sea creeping up to them, sucking at their boots and their guts. 'The best, lads.'

But the worst used, thought Ogilvie. If only the Regiment had got the posting to where Vin claimed he'd been. Korea. No way the brass hats could've disbanded a regiment that had done well there. As it was, the biggest thing the Regiment had been involved in after the Hitler war was Palestine.

Sammy Abercrombie always said they were jinxed from then on and he had bought himself out as soon as the rumours began to fly from the orderly room. And the Regiment was broken piece meal to fill the ranks of mobs without half its battle honours. Sammy Abercrombie was right. They were jinxed after Palestine. Aye, maybe jinxed from way back on Calvary.

Ogilvie put the dingo scalp hairy side down on a rock and rolled the scalp up before tucking it in his belt. Still, if it hadn't been for Palestine ... He rubbed the long, bruise-like mark on his right arm. Palestine and Shug Rodd moaning to get to midnight Mass.

83

Ogilvie moved to the river. He should've followed Sammy Abercrombie's example instead of volunteering for the Special Independent Counter Insurgency Company. He began to wash his hands in the river. Aye, maybe. But he was on the limit of his twenty-two years with the colours. And McAskill was clever. He had room for twenty-two-year men. 'Insurgents expect special forces to be young, Ogilvie. Veterans like yourself can be invaluable in certain areas of operation.'

Certain areas. McAskill lectured on the lessons of the jungles. Malaya. Borneo. Even Vietnam. But when the time came, it was into the jungles of Ireland he led them.

In the river, Ogilvie's face was reflected featureless. Tiny fish came to tug at the blood clots he was washing from his hands where the blood clots floated free of his featureless face. In it, Ogilvie saw Rodd's face appear, the eyes puzzled, mad, pleading: get me out of here. Get me home.

A stone hit the reflection, shattering the memory.

Up on the east side of the gorge, Sheean had Ogilvie in the rifle sights.

'Do it,' Ogilvie shouted, his voice caught and thrown back to him by the side of the gorge. An asylum perimeter wall. 'Do it. But get to me before the round. I don't want to die like like a dingo.'

He waited, unmoving. Sheean held on him. Might as well be damned as a murderer as a thief. God's life or God's loot. What odds? The foresight wavered. Sheean laid the rifle down. 'To hell with you, you big Presbo comedian. To hell with you.'

Ogilvie advanced into the river. 'Hell's not your business,' he shouted.

'No, booze is,' Sheean laughed. 'Postcoital booze. I'm for the pub.'

As Sheean went crashing off through the scrub, Ogilvie came out of the water. He stuck his bayonet in the ground and made a

84

mark next to its shadow. Give Vin an inch but he couldn't take a mile at a run. Wasn't fit enough. Not that there weren't fit ones. Stilwell, the padre, for one, doing his parachute jumps in the morning and then going back up in the afternoon to jump again as an encouragement to the first refusers.

Ogilvie stretched out on the ground and closed his eyes. Could go his whisky, too. Stilwell by all accounts. Nose on him you could warm your hands at. But he did his best work with water.

The shadow of Ogilvie's bayonet moved towards its mark. He dreamed of the colonel-in-chief he had loved from the first time he had seen her. He dreamed they were getting married. And Stilwell stood in front of them, draped in a white parachute. But the parachute turned to water and Stilwell was saying, '*Ego te baptizo* ... I baptise thee Alexander John Ogilvie. In the name of the Father and of the Son and of the Holy Ghost.'

Ogilvie awoke when the bayonet shadow was exactly on the mark he had made. Another of McAskill's tricks that: your body sleeps not your mind. Set your mind a time and it will waken your body.

The river caught the sun. Ogilvie stooped and cupped water in his hands, first to drink and then, remembering his dream, to splash on his head. Oh Christ, he thought. If not you, who?

Files hummed over the dingo carcase. Ogilvie thrust his bayonet into its scabbard and began to climb the gorge face. First objective: his rifle. Second objective: Vin.

24

Bel Maley laid another bundle of brushwood on top of the corrugated-iron roof of the house and turned to get another from Bobbie who was passing to them from the top of the ladder.

'All gone,' he said. 'Smoko time.'

She gave the bundle a final thump with the flat of her hand. One side nearly covered and when the whole roof was, it would be nice and cool inside. Allersame a gunyah. Allersame the other one. She moved carefully backwards on the ladder.

Bobbie, moving down himself, guided her bare feet onto the top rung. Suddenly, joy broke in Bel like the waters of a new birth. A funny kid, her Bobbie, kissing his mumma's feet while they were on a ladder.

Her other kids were waiting round a fire near what they were already calling 'Og's Gunyah'. A big damper of flour, baking powder and water was waiting in the ashes of the fire. Bel dusted it off, blowing on it and broke it into pieces. She spread jam on the pieces and passed them out to her kids. Bobbie was pouring tea from a billycan with a spout into plastic mugs.

Bel leant over and wiped Enid's nose with her thumb and forefinger.

'Story,' said Enid.

All the kids laughed because Enid had sounded funny speaking through her pinched-in nose.

'Yair,' said Johnny. 'Long story.'

Bel munched on her piece of damper, took a sup of tea and began, 'One time ...'

In her mind, another language moved like the memory of a miscarried child in her womb.

'Long time ago, Missus Emu and Missus Bush Turkey each had a nice family of bubbas.'

'Allersame you, eh?' said Johnny.

Bel handed him another piece of damper. 'You be smart, you listen. You learn. Long time ago. Dream time ago. Then one day Missus Emu went walkabout and when she came back she only had one bubba. "Where you put 'im others," said Missus Bush Turkey.

'"Oh," said Missus Emu, "They been too much plurry trouble.

86

I been got rid of them. All the time hungry. All the time cry. I'm surprised you put up with so many yourself, my dear. They're restricting your development as a person." '

'Really and truly?'

'Oath, darl. She was Missus White Emu.'

Bobbie held out his hand, 'Sounds more like one of those funny old government cows that was up here last year.'

Bel gave him the last piece of damper. 'You keep quiet. The littlies want to hear.'

'I want to know how you know the story,' said Harold.

'Because Mr Eagle was circling round the whole time they were yabbering and he told your grandpa. He was eagle. Well then, Missus Bush Turkey thought it over. So she went walkabout and killed all her bubbas.'

'No,' said Enid. 'No.'

Bel lifted Enid onto her lap, wiped her nose and put her to her breast. She noticed Olga and waved her into her lap as well and continued, 'Missus Bush Turkey was a real dill because Missus Emu went and got the rest of her bubbas from where she had hidden them.

'Missus Bush Turkey dropped her bundle when she realised she had been humbugged. She sang Missus Emu. Ever since emus haven't been able to fly and their droppings have been extra big to show how much bullshit they talk.'

Harold laughed. 'Too much humbug, that story.'

Bel reached to cuff him. He rolled out of her reach and ran off. Bel said to Bobbie, 'He needs belting properly.'

Bobbie licked his fingers. 'Maybe that balanda Vin belt him. Or Ogilvie.'

Bel shook her head. Bobbie smiled, his big, white teeth shining, 'Boondoo belt him. That Harold needs belting. I belt him. Found him sniffing petrol.'

'He needs belting properly.'

Bobbie said, 'Og's idea all about fixing up these houses into gunyahs. Turning on water. Not the fire.'

'You're eagle allersame grandpa.'

'Horse me,' said Bobbie, 'not eagle.'

'You been riding that horse belong Boondoo,' said Bel.

'I ride him more better, me. Faster.'

Boondoo go away and horses.'

'Maybe I go. Boondoo horse. Me horse.'

Olga began to cry. Bel hugged her. 'Your dad, he'll come back by and by. You'll see.'

25

Des Parkes gripped the icicle more tightly. Ought to stick it in his belly. No, his brain, the way he was thinking.

He restarted his check on the grog supplies. Three dozen of beer but no worries; Vodka and Sudan would be on the way back by now with reinforcements from Yelboom. One dozen and three bottles of whisky. Two dozen champagne. Five dozen brandy. Four dozen and eleven rum. So that was where the bottle in the flag cupboard had come from. Seven bottles of gin and six of that hangover cure with the name nobody could pronounce.

Might need those before this bloke Halliday was finished. A real booze artist by all accounts. Good of Tim Webster to bring him through. Once the word got round that Tembo Halliday had been in Rainbow, there would be others. Yanks. Plenty of them. The more the merrier. And the quicker the government might lash out on a mile or two of bitumen.

Then Mary would give up her idea of moving to Yelboom. They could even employ Bel again. He looked at his hand. The icicle had melted. His hand was cold. Not the rest of him. Bel. The size of her compared to Mary. The abundance. The liveliness. And Mary was as pale as a taper. That combo bastard was right. He had put the hard word on Bel. What else could a bloke do? Mary Down Below in hospital having her tit off and Bel all over the place. Two hands full. And running over.

He broke another icicle off the water pipe which ran through the boiler room. Must be a leak somewhere. Typical Grandpa Jim lash-up. Converting the old boiler room into a cold room. Cost a fortune. Helped to kill him. What a way to go. Pneumonia with the outside temperature at 120. Drowning in a drought, thinking his horse had at last won the Rainbow Picnic Races.

'I'll do it for you, Grandpa Jim,' Des Parkes whispered. 'I've got the horses.' He blew on his hands and took a folded sheet of paper from the back pocket of his shorts. The receipt signed by Boondoo and sealed with a beer stain.

Des Parkes grew very still. Someone was moving upstairs. Not Mary. She did not creep about. Or clink bottles. Very quietly, Des Parkes closed the insulated door of the main boiler.

By the time he got up the stairs, he was out of breath. But when he heard the bottles clinking again and saw that blue backside, he swung his foot. Vin Sheean went head first into the cold cupboard. He emerged holding his head and bottle of port. Des Parkes grabbed the bottle.

'Out,' he shouted, 'out. Coming to it when a bloke can't check his supplies without some bludger trying to rob him blind.'

He advanced on Sheean holding the bottle of port by the neck.

Sheean raised his hands, open and outstretched. 'Fair go, Des. I knew you were busy. So I was helping myself.'

Des Parkes put the bottle of port back in the cold cupboard and slammed the door. 'You're not having that.'

Sheean said, 'Bloody boong juice. Didn't want it. Wanted a beer. You got to me before I could get to it.'

'Out.' Des Parkes grabbed him. 'No beer. Out.'

'I can pay.' Sheean fumbled in his overall pocket, trying to peel a banknote from the wad.

Des Parkes pushed him towards the door. 'You'll pay. That's for sure, you bludger. I'm going to kick you back to where you belong.'

Sheean resisted, trying to jab his elbow into Des Parkes's belly. 'You haven't got that much kick in you.'

They were still struggling when Ogilvie came into the pub. He propped his rifle in a corner and watched them. The Blubberweight Shoving and Pushing Championship of the World. He took a step towards the bar.

'My shout,' he said.

Des Parkes kept pushing Sheean towards the door. 'Your mate said he would pay. Thieving mongrel.'

Sheean got his hand out of his pocket. It was empty. He tried to reach Des Parkes's throat. 'Ikey bastard. Won't even trust a bloke for a drink.'

'I'll show you how far I trust you,' said Des Parkes. 'Thieving mongrel. You've slept with so many lubras, you've picked up more than their fleas.'

'Liar.'

'It's the truth. And you don't want to hear the truth.'

'No more than you.' Sheean twisted round. 'No more than anyone. He punched Des Parkes in the face. Des Parkes gasped, 'I'll –'

Ogilvie reached over the bar and got a grip on Sheean. 'Some mate you are. Leaving me on my tod so you can come back here and sneak a grog.'

Des Parkes said, 'Same as he did when he got out of jail ahead of you.'

90

Sheean struggled to free himself. 'I didn't ask him to get himself inside. He was supposed to be on his way home. I've told him and I'm telling you. I got myself jailed for a bit of a rest.. Next thing he's inside with me.'

Des Parkes went into reverse, trying to pull Sheean away from Ogilvie, trying and saying, 'Don't know why you bother with the bastard, Og. You should've let those miners do him.'

'Couldn't.' Ogilvie lifted Sheean half across the bar. 'Needed him.'

'Flaming hell,' said Sheean, 'you blokes'll have me coming apart at the seams.'

He struggled more violently, yelling. Ogilvie heaved him right across the bar. Rodd. Rodd had fought silently so as not to wake his son.

Des Parkes, looking up at Ogilvie, wondered whether even Grandpa Jim would have been mighty enough to throw him out. He let go of Sheean.

'Thieving mongrel. I don't want you coming apart at the seams,' he said. 'You'd leave shit all over the floor.'

Sheean stood up on the bar and danced along it before jumping to the floor.

Des Parkes said, 'If I catch you on my side of the bar again.'

Sheean did not reply. Ogilvie waved the dingo scalp. 'My shout.' Des Parkes tried to stare him out. In the silence, they all heard the horse and knew that Boondoo, as he did every Sunday, was walking Lubra past the empty schoolhouse to the signpost which said 'Melbourne 1600 miles' before galloping her back to the pub.

'Mad boong,' said Des Parkes.

Sheean said, 'That's not the way you were talking last night.'

'The round,' said Ogilvie, 'the round. Get the round in.'

Des Parkes put up two cans of beer and opened another for himself. 'Thieving mongrel. Drink that beer and get out.'

91

'Whisper it, Des. I can hear you better when you whisper. Like last night with Boondoo.'

'Shut up, drink up and get out.'

'Sorry, Des, I can drink up and shut up and get out but I can't shut up, drink up and get out.'

'Drink up then.'

'All right. If you insist.' Sheean swallowed the last of his beer and put the empty can on the bar. 'I will have another to celebrate the deal.'

'Shut up. I was doing him a favour. A boong. What could he do? Really? Mad as a brush. Him and his idea.'

'Oh, I don't know,' said Sheean. 'The first winner of the Melbourne Cup was walked a long, long way to the race course.'

Grinning, he turned as Boondoo came through the door, 'Isn't that right, mate? Wasn't Archer, first winner of the Melbourne Cup, walked all the way to the race course?'

Boondoo nodded and adjusted the long stockwhip looped over his shoulder. He could not understand why balandas asked questions about things they already knew.

Des Parkes said to Sheean, 'You're nothing but a stirrer and the sooner you're out of here the better.'

Sheean bowed his head. 'Amen to that but what about another beer?'

'Beer.' Des Parkes took a can from the cold cupboard. Sheean reached for it and Parkes shoved it in his face. Sheean reeled back, his nose bleeding. Parkes handed the can to Boondoo, who put it on the bar and backed away, shaking his head.

'Aw, look,' said Des Parkes, 'I told you last night you were on free grog. And your money's safe.'

Boondoo shook his head.

'But if you want it now.' From under the bar, Des Parkes took a battered syrup tin, opened it and produced a roll of banknotes,

92

tied together with an old bootlace. He held the roll out to Boondoo who came forward again. Sheean, too, moved towards the roll of notes.

'Christ knows,' he laughed. 'When I last saw a roll that size.'

'Hands off,' said Des Parkes. 'Thieving mongrel.'

Ogilvie thumped on the bar with his fist. 'Hell's going on?'

Sheean laughed again. 'You really wiped yourself out last night, mate. Missed the deal of the century. Boondoo sold his horses to Des here for two thousand and –'

Ogilvie roared, 'He didn't.'

'Free grog for life.'

'And I've got a receipt to prove it.' Des Parkes took out the folded paper and handed it to Ogilvie. He watched warily while Ogilvie studied the receipt, refolded it and put it back on the bar, smiling.

'This calls for a celebration. Beers all round,' said Ogilvie, 'and what about some potato chips?'

Des Parkes got the beers out. Boondoo watched Ogilvie as Des Parkes placed a packet of potato chips on the bar. Ogilvie ripped open the packet. Des Parkes turned to get himself a rum. Ogilvie put his hand in the packet of chips. He turned to Boondoo, holding out the packet of chips. 'Salted,' he said.

Boondoo glanced from Ogilvie to Des Parkes.

Ogilvie shook the packet. 'Go on, mate. Go on. It's your celebration.'

Boondoo stared at Ogilvie. 'Take some,' said Ogilvie. 'Take a good handful.'

'Yeah,' said Des Parkes, 'hop in. Or I will.'

Boondoo put the handful of potato chips in his mouth and began to chew.

'And another thing,' said Des Parkes, 'I want you to keep looking after those horses for me.'

93

'Right, boss.' Boondoo chewed on.

Des Parkes said, 'Better take your money before I change my mind.' He laughed. 'You drove a real hard bargain.'

Boondoo shook his head, still chewing. Ogilvie opened a can of beer and gave it to him. 'Your last,' he said, 'if you're going to win the cup and show wee Olga what her dad's made of.'

'Bloody nonsense,' said Des Parkes. 'He can forget all that. They're my horses now. They're staying up here for the Picnic Races. The Rainbow Cup. Myall's going to win that for me. Not the flaming Melbourne bloody Cup.'

Boondoo shook his head and washed down what was left in his mouth with the beer. He turned for the door. A good beer that last one.

'Your money,' said Des Parkes.

Boondoo stood framed in the doorway, all black and never taller. 'Stickitass, balanda.'

Sheean added, 'Which being interpreted means "Stick it up your arse, whiteman", balanda being a corruption of Hollander, a description of the Dutch who were among the first Europeans to visit these shores.'

Des Parkes reached for the wooden mallet once used to drive spigots into barrels. 'I know what he means and if he's not careful I'll stick this in his skull to show how empty it is.' He thumped the mallet down on the bar. 'Bloody boong and his bloody idea. What would he know about the Melbourne Cup? The money it takes to enter. Grog's all he knows.'

Boondoo said, 'I know one thing, boss. No plurry receipt. No plurry deal.'

Des Parkes thumped the mallet on the bar again. 'But I've got a receipt, you cheeky bastard. The receipt you signed.' He looked along the bar. 'It's here.' He leant over the bar to look on the floor. 'Somewhere.'

Ogilvie said, 'You seen it, Boondoo?'

Boondoo shook his head. 'Number one tucker those chips.'

'Stop yabbering on about tucker,' Des Parkes shouted, 'I want that flaming receipt.'

'No receipt. No deal,' said Ogilvie. 'Boondoo's right.'

Des Parkes pushed the roll of notes on the bar. 'There's more there than you've seen in your life, Boondoo. And don't forget the free grog. Any time.'

'No more grog, boss. No more.'

Sheean stretched out his hand to take the roll of notes. 'If no one wants it.'

Des Parkes slammed the mallet down on Sheean's hand. 'Leave it, you thieving mongrel.'

Sheean howled in pain. If thy hand scandalise you, have it smashed by a publican and sinner with a wooden mallet.

And Des Parkes yelled, 'I've got a deal and a receipt. Some-where.'

Ogilvie said, 'Any witnesses?'

'I don't want you sticking your bib in,' said Des Parkes. 'This is my business and Boondoo's.'

'Aye,' said Ogilvie. 'And it's mine too. Bondoo's a mate. And we were drinking together last night.'

Boondoo rubbed his head. 'Bad night, boss. I don't remember all that much.'

'Listen,' said Des Parkes.

'Can't, boss. Got to exercise Lubra. Got a long way to go, Lubra and me and Myall.'

'For God's sake.' Des Parkes's voice rose to a scream. 'Listen, there's no way in the world you can win the Cup. No way you can enter. No way you can even get there.'

'Can walk, boss,' said Boondoo. And did, the loops of his stock whip curled round his shoulder.

Ogilvie crumpled the potato-chip packet into a ball, dropped it and kicked it on the half volley through the door. 'Easy!' he shouted. 'Easy! Sergeant Death.'

26

Tembo Halliday guffawed as he twisted the hinge remaining on the door of the ramshackle latrine which stood like a sentry box by the side of the road.

Watching him through the telephoto lens of one of his cameras and clicking off shots, Ashby was sure Halliday had gone mad. Between guffaws, he was shouting, 'I've got to have it. This is it. Final goddamn word on Shakespeare, Tolstoy, Balzac, Browning, Stendhal, Dickens and his sob sister Marie Corelli. Final goddamn word.'

The door came off the hinge with a squeal of drawn nails. Like me, thought Halliday, only I couldn't squeal loud enough and staggered back to the four-wheel drive carrying the door.

'Don't stand there taking happy snaps,' he said to Ashby. 'File this with the rest of your archive.'

'File it?'

'That's why you're along, goddamn it. To file and type and tape and take happy snaps.'

Donaldson held out his water bag to Sue Cornwall. 'I thought you were the secretary.'

She moved away from him to stand next to Tim Webster who was saying. 'No shortages of firewood here.'

'Not firewood.' Halliday swung the door round so that the inside faced Webster.

On it, someone had scrawled, 'People who need paper are the loneliest people in the world.'

Halliday said, 'Genius touch. Total genius. Writing that with finger dipped in shit.' He guffawed again. 'Yeah. What's writing but finger dipped in ego shit.'

Webster grinned. 'Well, you said it, Tembo. But that door. Fact is, I don't think we can take it with us.'

Ashby switched to another camera and clicked off a shot of the door. Halliday shoved the door at him. 'It's this I want. File it. On the roof.'

Webster said, 'Sorry, Tembo. I try to oblige my customers. But a shithouse door.'

'Your contract calls for you to carry me and any trophies.'

'Shithouse doors aren't trophies.'

Halliday turned to Ashby. 'Take it back.'

Ashby lifted the door and started back to the latrine with it. Webster said to Donaldson, 'Give him a hand, mate.'

Donaldson said, 'His job. Not mine. And it's only about a hundred yards.'

'Should make you walk the rest of the way to Rainbow,' said Webster, moving to help Ashby.

Halliday prevented him. 'Ash may be weak but he's clever. Right?'

Ashby now began dragging the door towards the latrine. Halliday picked up his rifle and said to Webster, 'In the mood for a little shooting match?'

Webster said, 'Nothing worth shooting. Few rabbits. Roos.'

'The door. Bullet through it makes it trophy within meaning of contract.'

Webster pulled at his nose as if trying to tug it out by the roots. He knew customers were inclined to go a bit strange when they joined him for a trip. Well, not so much strange. More childish. But this was no child. 'Listen,' said Webster. 'There's better than shithouse doors waiting.'

97

'I've shot better than what's waiting. Lion, ever shoot lion? Lion comes gliding at you, man, it's adrenalin highball time. Leopard. Elephant. Rhino. Buffalo. Black African buffalo. Shot them all. Big five. Now I want to shoot me a shithouse door.'

Webster tried grinning again. 'Man who can't hit a shithouse door would have to be blind drunk.'

Ashby was propping the door back in position against the latrine. Halliday shouted, 'Other way round, Fisi.' And said to Webster, 'I put bullet through O of first "people", we take it. I miss and you put hole through O of second "people", we leave it and I pay you bonus of one hundred dollars.'

Webster went to the four-wheel drive to get his rifle. If Tembo Halliday wanted to throw money around.

Halliday swung his telescopic sight onto the doorway. Then onto Ashby, who was halfway back to the four-wheel drive. He fired. The round kicked earth to Ashby's right. He froze. Halliday shouted, 'Told you the other way round. I want that door inside out so's I can see the inscription.' He fired again and Ashby collapsed.

Sue Cornwall screamed. Halliday guffawed. 'He's OK. Gun-shy without his camera is all.' He added to Donaldson, 'Door. Turn it round.'

Donaldson was trotting towards the latrine before he thought of telling the Yank to rack off. He slowed to a walk instead. Yanks. They were spitting you out before you realised they'd sucked you in. He turned the door round so that its inscription faced outwards.

Webster came back to Halliday from the four-wheel drive, loading a rifle.

'Mauser,' said Halliday. 'Fine weapon. Prefer my Savage.' He held up his rifle so that the sun took its inlaid butt and gleamed along its barrel.

Sue Cornwall smiled. Like two big kids comparing toys.

On the way back from the latrine, Donaldson stopped to help Ashby up. Halliday noted the drift of the dust from their feet and glanced at the door. When Ashby and Donaldson were behind him, Halliday sighted on the O. Stillness flowed into him. And peace. Stubbled fields and frost. White breath and blue gunsmoke. His daddy's belief that there was no pain so great it could not be borne. His mama's that there was no pain. All in the mind. Halliday held on the O, putting the pain from his body into his mind to plug it into the O.

At the moment he squeezed off the round, an energy beyond pain split him into an incandescent agony. He fell to his knees. His rifle barrel went skywards and the bullet carried the agony from him: Take that, God. It's too much for me.

Ashby's camera clicked and whirred. Donaldson laughed. 'Typical bloody Yank. Can't even hit a shithouse door.' He touched Sue Cornwall. 'How'd he get a hold of you?'

Halliday swung his rifle onto Donaldson and levered a fresh round into the breech. Tim Webster stepped between them. 'My go,' he said, brought his rifle up and fired. The bullet cracked into the door, right on the second O.

'You've got one hundred coming to you,' said Halliday, getting to his feet.

'No hurry,' said Webster, putting a second round into the first O.

'Good on the Aussie,' said Donaldson to Sue Cornwall. Quietly.

Not quietly enough for Halliday, who knew he needed an animal more dangerous than any he'd ever shot. He fronted Donaldson saying, 'You shoot mouth off pretty good. How about this?' And prodded Donaldson in the stomach with the rifle butt.

He sensed Donaldson getting set for a punch in the shifting of his feet and the shiver of a muscle on his forearm. He held Donaldson's eyes with his. It would take more than a punch. He prodded Donaldson again with the rifle butt.

Donaldson knew he could drop the old coot, rifle or no rifle. Yeah, take the rifle and give him a taste of more than the butt. What he couldn't take was the weird appeal in the old coot's blue eyes.

'Rack off,' said Donaldson turning away from Halliday and going to the four-wheel drive.

Webster moved, too. 'Yeah. Rainbow's waiting. Cold showers and colder beer.'

Halliday said, 'Sounds good,' put his rifle to his shoulder, sighted on the shithouse door and fired. His bullet cracked and ripped through the O of 'who'.

He laughed then and Ashby got another shot of him. He shoved Ashby towards the four-wheel drive.

'Are you okay, Tembo?' said Ashby.

'Sure, Fisi, sure,' said Halliday, prodding him with his rifle. 'Hyena time not yet.'

27

Vodka Mahonsky spotted Boondoo on Lubra before Sudan O'Brien which annoyed Sudan. Then, as Boondoo rode towards the tractor trailer in which they were sitting, Vodka fumbled for the clasp knife pouched on his belt. He pulled a beer carton towards him, meaning to rip the top off and give Boondoo a drink.

Sudan took over the carton. 'Won't tell you again, you mug reffo.' He turned the beer carton upside down, eased back the flaps and took out two cans. 'No more than two cans from each carton,' he said. 'Time Des finds out, we may have some money to pay for them.'

As Boondoo dismounted, Sudan jumped from the trailer. Lubra shied away to the full extent of her reins. Sudan took off his hat, opened a can of beer and poured it into his hat. He passed the hat of beer to Boondoo who offered it to Lubra. The horse drank greedily.

Up on the trailer, Vodka opened another carton from the bottom. He held out a can of beer to Boondoo, who shook his head. Sudan stared at him in surprise and opened a can for himself. Bloody boongs. Never knew which way they were going to go – even wowser. Time was when a man could have had his pick of the gins for a pannikin of grog.

Vodka drank, stretching his feet out so that they rested against one of the bags of ice packed round the beer. He closed his eyes. Strange thing. He could now imagine the look of the snow but he could not truly recall the cold.

He opened his eyes to squint at the hand clutching the cold beer can. The top joints of two of his fingers were missing. Yet the cold had bitten them off.

Boondoo said, 'You blokes going to try for that fencing contract?'

'Fencing contract,' said Sudan.

Vodka waved his can. 'Meant to say. Boondoo heard there was a fencing contract. Big one.'

'So why didn't you tell me, you mug reffo. Me. Your mate.'

'On Mundarra.'

Sudan climbed onto the hub of the trailer wheel and thrust his face at Vodka. 'Mundarra. You should have said so in the first place. You know I can't work on Mundarra.'

Vodka nodded, smiling. Everyone knew Sudan had got across the management of Mundarra years ago. Everyone knew he had been told he would never work on the station again. Everyone knew why: because Sudan tried to get a mob of blacks living on Mundarra to help muster cattle on Rainbow Downs when old man Parkes still had it. Everyone knew what the manager of Mundarra had told him. Everyone knew because Sudan told everyone. Sometimes more than once as he was doing now, 'And do you know what that bastard Franklyn told me, that jumped up book-keeper? Know what he said?'

Sudan, in his rage forgetting his instruction to Vodka, leant into the trailer and took a third can from the bottom of the open carton. 'Know what that jumped-up book-keeper said. To me. Sudan O'Brien, first to lead them and head them. He said, that jumped-up book-keeper, that big bosses' bum-licker, he said, "We took care of Peron in the Argentine. Don't think we can't take care of a bolshy bastard like you, O'Brien."'

He looked at the unopened can in his hand. 'I'll show him.' He opened the can and drank it off in one. Up on the trailer, Vodka turned the beer cartons right way up and repacked the ice bags around them.

Sudan turned to Boondoo. 'I'll take Lubra. You go with Vodka on the tractor.'

It was a request by the time he got it out. Boondoo gave him the reins. Sudan mounted. A man should never have given horses away. No fun squatting on a stinking tractor or riding in a ute when a man could be up and seeing all the way to the curve of the earth. He touched Lubra with his heels. She began to buck. He held onto her and she twisted sideways, going forward at the same time.

Sudan was on the track looking up into the laughing face of Vodka who was saying, 'Not so good ride a drunk horse when you are drunk, mate.'

Lubra was standing stock still and Boondoo was in the saddle into which he had leapt as soon as Sudan fell.

Sudan got to his feet. 'Last one back into the pub buys the beer.'

'We have no money,' said Vodka, starting to edge across the tow bar towards the tractor. Sudan beat him to the driving seat. 'My credit's good,' he said, 'I'm no blow-in who got here only because he bumped into Australia while trying to get to America from bloody Russia.'

Vodka moved back to the trailer. It was a mistake to tell anyone anything. He ought to have learnt that. He wedged the ends of the gidgee poles under the cartons of beer and packed the bags of ice more firmly.

Sudan started the tractor, shouting to Boondoo, 'Little bet. Ten, say?'

'Twenty,' said Boondoo.

'Give us a start?'

'How far?'

'First gate,' said Sudan.

Boondoo nodded.

'Through first gate,' said Sudan.

Boondoo could see the first gate. Not more than 300 yards away. And there were four more between them and Rainbow. Maybe a couple of miles all up. 'Fair enough,' said Boondoo.

The tractor roared off. Lubra shied and shied again at the red rag on the end of the gidgee poles.

28

Sue Cornwall woke in the roaring four-wheel drive to the clicking of Ashby's camera and his 'Oh my God, I don't believe it's real.'

She saw, as brightly as a childhood dream, what he was seeing: the pub at Rainbow floating on a blue mirage.

'Oh, my God,' Ashby said again.

Halliday, switching on his tape recorder, said, 'Shut up' and into the tape recorder, 'To traverse the Outback of Australia is to become figure in landscape where ordinary is mirage changed, pub transformed into ark of new covenant which you dare not try to touch because you can't believe it is solid.'

Tim Webster said, 'She's solid all right. Real. Real as a beer.'

And exactly what he needed to make his Ausafaris work. He could see that now. These Yanks needed their comforts. Only soldiers in the world to use banana-flavoured grease on their bayonets, as his old mate Blue used to say.

Ashby leant out of the window and continued to click off shots. Halliday went on talking to himself by way of the tape recorder: 'Australia then, it seems to me, is first country in history to go from penal colony to client state without drawing truly independent breath. Americans, whose country was born in defiance and nurtured in courage, may find it difficult to conceive of whole continent whose challenge has been met in terms of convict cowardice and with cry to wide world, "Will someone please be our warder?" This cry –'

Webster stamped on the brake pedal. Bloody Yank. The four-wheel drive slewed to a halt. Halliday raised the hand holding the tape recorder to stop his head going through the windscreen.

'Shit and derision,' he said as the tape recorder smashed against the windscreen.

Webster, whose arm had come across to hold Sue Cornwall, said, 'Sorry, Tembo. Should've reminded you to fasten your seat belt.'

'Maybe. But why the panic stop?'

'No panic, Tembo. Bad luck to run over a snake.'

'Didn't see any snake.'

'Shot off into the bush. Big bloke. Very bad luck to run over him.'

Halliday examined his tape recorder, switching the buttons on and off. 'Move it,' he said to Webster and into the tape recorder, 'One of odd superstitions of Australian back country is that running over snake brings bad luck. Bigger snake, bigger bad luck. Leave it to professional anthropologists to establish whether superstition is related to ancient, aboriginal cult of Rainbow Snake.'

Webster smiled, restarted the four-wheel drive and said, 'Better fasten your seat belt.'

Halliday ignored the suggestion. He put the tape recorder back in his pocket. Crazy, the way he had used it to stop himself going through the windscreen when what he needed was a blade of glass smack in the jugular.

29

Sudan had to slow the tractor to let Vodka off to open the first cattle gate. 'Give it an extra twist,' he shouted. 'Delay the bastard.'

Vodka double-twisted the loop of wire round the metal pipe which secured the gate. Sudan had the tractor moving again while Vodka was still climbing into the trailer. Vodka scarcely managed to roll over the tail gate. He lay for a moment, head resting against a bag of ice. That's where he ought to be. In the cold, outlasting the stupid Communists. But the sun was so good here, and life. Childhood again but better. He peeped over the tail gate. Boondoo had started his run, moving beautifully with his horse as Vodka had once seen rank upon rank of men moving with their horses against tanks.

Crawling to the front of the trailer, Vodka shouted, 'He's after us.'

Sudan accelerated. 'He'll stay after us.' Vodka peered back through the dust. Boondoo was coming up on them, faster than a ghost. But he would have to dismount to open the gate.

Vodka was wrong. Boondoo did not dismount. He took Lubra straight at the gate. They went up and over. Vodka saw sparks fly as Lubra's hoofs struck flints on the road. 'He has jumped the gate,' he shouted.

Sudan twisted round to have a look. The tractor veered off the track into a water run-off cut. As Sudan fought the tractor and trailer back onto the track, Vodka sprawled sideways.

The train had gone sideways, screeching steam and spilling him and the rest of the fencing squad from the huddled warmth of their cattle truck into the sudden cold of that snow-lit night.

Vodka lay in the rattling trailer, thinking of what his mate, Sudan, had said about his bumping into Australia on the way to America. Sudan was right because he had told Sudan he had been aiming for America when he walked away from the train smash and a future of extra rations for wrapping men and women in the wire of Siberia.

He had told Sudan how he killed the guard who tried to stop him, killed the guard with a roll of barbed wire and took his clothes, leaving brains and blood to freeze on the snow as black as a child's idea of sin.

Vodka crunched a chunk of ice. A man had to tell someone what he knew God knew or go mad, as Ogilvie was going mad with whatever it was God knew about him.

30

Tim Webster accelerated the four-wheel drive into the long straight leading to the Rainbow turn-off. Sooner he got this mob under a cold shower and outside a cold beer the better. Though the way this coot Halliday was behaving, more cold shower than cold beer would be in order. Might even be an idea to get them straight to the camp and not overnight in Rainbow. Des Parkes would be ropeable, and Mary, but he'd make it up to them.

'Been thinking,' said Webster, slowing to match his drawl, 'maybe we should just give Rainbow a good day and hurroo.'

'You mean no overnight?' said Halliday.

'Faster we get to the camp, Tembo, faster we're hunting,' said Webster. 'We can be out at first light tomorrow.'

Halliday's hand went to Sue Cornwall's thigh. 'You want that we should get straight on, Bibi?'

'You're here to hunt, aren't you?

As soon as she said this, Sue Cornwall knew she should've insisted on overnighting to make Halliday go straight on. He said, 'Make it a rule to recce new hunting ground in full daylight, Tim. We overnight.' He squeezed Sue Cornwall's thigh. 'Give the con-demned man a chance to have a hearty wench.'

Sue Cornwall said nothing. If she didn't play his game, she didn't lose. He squeezed her thigh again, his hand higher. 'Hear what I said?'

'I can't hear anything.' She took a cigarette lighter from her handbag. 'Or feel anything.'

'Got to give the condemned man a chance to have a hearty wench,' Halliday said. And when she didn't reply. 'Tell you some-thing.'

Behind Halliday, Ashby switched on his tape recorder as Halli-day continued, 'You're my last, Bibi. Wish you were my first. There again, wish I hadn't laid my first, then I'd remember her. Women you remember best are ones you didn't lay. So maybe shouldn't've laid you because sure as hell want to remember you.'

She clicked on the gold lighter. 'Your mind's wandering.' She brought the flame down. 'So is your hand.'

He took his hand from her thigh. 'Pain. It doesn't exist except in the mind.' He held his hand over the lighter flame and began counting, 'One, two, three, four, five.' She clicked off the lighter.

'See what I mean?' he said. 'Your mind couldn't bear the pain in my mind.'

107

She scrabbled in her handbag, found a cigarette and lit it. 'I couldn't stand the smell of you cooking,' she said.

Ashby laughed. Halliday said, 'Thought you were fixing to have me raw, Fisi. All sliced up in a leather-bound sandwich.'

'You're too tough for me, Tembo,' said Ashby.

'Not after I've been hung for a day or three. Be high and tender for little, old hyena like you, Fisi.'

Ashby moved his tape recorder closer to Halliday, holding it high and clear of the front seat. 'It's your opinion on Australia, not me, the public want.'

Halliday twisted round in his seat and took a punch at the tape recorder, knocking it from Ashby's hand to the back of the four-wheel drive. 'If you want to tape me, Fisi, don't annoy me like some goddamn clipboard creep on television.'

3 1

Boondoo and Lubra were closing the gap between them and the tractor and trailer in a blur of hoofbeats. Boondoo swung Lubra to pass on the nearside so as to get the benefit of the inside track on the curves ahead. Sudan caught a glimpse of him in the rearview mirror and swung the steering wheel to whip the trailer across Boondoo's line of approach, yelling, 'Mug boong, you're not fit to ride a hobbyhorse on a hurdy-gurdy.'

Boondoo had to pull up. As he did, he felt the offside rein break and was flung forward on Lubra's neck.

The second gate, wavering in the heat shimmer, appeared ahead of the tractor and trailer.

'Jump,' Sudan shouted to Vodka.

'Too fast.'

'Jump.' Sudan slowed the tractor. Vodka jumped from the trailer and hit the track running towards the gate. He swung the gate open. The tractor roared through and Vodka simply pushed the gate closed without fastening it before leaping for the moving trailer and clambering aboard it.

Boondoo had kept Lubra going and was now trying to thread the end of his stockwhip through the snaffle ring to improvise a new rein. He succeeded on the third attempt but could not risk jumping Lubra over the second gate. He leant from the saddle, pulled the gate open, went through and from ingrained habit stopped to fasten the gate securely behind him.

Vodka could just see him from the back of the swaying trailer. 'He did not jump,' Vodka shouted and climbed out of the trailer to edge across the tow bar and stand beside Sudan.

'He doesn't jump the gates, we win,' said Sudan, looking up at Vodka. 'Just leave things to me.'

'Watch road,' said Vodka.

'I told you leave it to me, you reffo. And do what I tell you, when I tell you.'

'You want beer?'

'No, I don't. I want your weight back in the trailer. She'll turn over otherwise.'

Vodka began edging back across the tow bar to the trailer. If Sudan didn't want beer, he would have two himself.

32

Ashby examined his tape recorder, did a testing-testing bit and playback to make sure it was still working. He looked out of the rear window to where a jumble of boulders waited for giants to bowl them at the termite towers. In London, it had all seemed so simple: travel with Tembo Halliday to Australia, the only continent he hadn't visited or killed in. Record his impressions. Take some pictures of him in the landscape. Put the transcripts and pictures together. Add four legs. Hey presto. Australia A–Z, the coffee-table book.

But Tembo wasn't really buying the idea although he'd been keen enough on the advance. Went sour on it in Sydney.

Ashby glanced in Sue Cornwall's direction. Was that because the woman had gone sour on Halliday? Shouldn't wonder. All that Bibi bit. As bad as the Fisi bit. And the bloody *nugu* bit. Swahili. Language of Tembo Halliday's greatest success. But Tembo was the bloody monkey. *Persona non grata* in more dialects than Swahili. Ashby switched on his tape recorder and whispered into it: 'New proverb out of Africa: never call the cable-office clerk "Bloody Nugu". He may be the next chief of the secret police and find out who your mistress is.'

'Japanese?' Donaldson shouted from where he sat on the other side of the vehicle. And, at Ashby's puzzlement, 'The tape recorder.'

Ashby nodded. 'Knew it,' said Donaldson. 'Saw one exactly the same when I was in Singapore a few years ago. Ever been there?'

Ashby nodded. 'Unbelievable, eh? The Japs. You wouldn't think that only recently they had to copy everything. Me dad told me they once built a boat which sank when they launched it because they forgot to put a bung in it.'

Ashby smiled. 'Folklore's alive and distorting,' he said.

Donaldson didn't get his drift. 'Yeah, the bung wasn't on the plans the Japs copied, apparently.'

'Amazing,' said Ashby.

'Too bloody right it is,' said Donaldson. 'Now look at them. Transistors, television sets, cameras, watches, cars. Everything. That a Jap camera?'

Ashby raised one of his cameras to his eye and focused it on Donaldson. Quite a good-looking boy. He clicked off a shot.

'Wouldn't mind a copy of that,' said Donaldson.

Ashby opened up another of his cameras and focused it on Donaldson. The flash exploded. Within seconds, Ashby, smiling, handed Donaldson a colour print of himself.

Donaldson didn't go for Ashby's smile. Bit of a poofdah, this bloke. The way he stared, too. Bit like the way the old bloke'd stared. Except the old bloke was asking for something different.

Staring at the photograph of himself, Donaldson said, 'Make a nice postcard for me mum. She'll be pleased to know I'm still in one piece.'

Ashby said, 'You should've stayed with your rig.'

Donaldson grinned. 'No way. Wasn't my rig. I was its driver. Its bloody slave. And the finance company's. I'm going to bore it right up the bastards and they won't be able to do a thing about it except smile.'

33

Boondoo crouched lower in the saddle and felt Lubra stretch out into a track-raking gallop as if the dust cloud from the tractor were a mob that had rushed.

He felt himself flow into her and she into him, telling him, telling him, telling him with every stride; telling him he need only jump the gates to win.

Vodka ran for the third gate, opened it and Sudan drove the tractor and trailer through. This time he stopped, left the engine running and jumped from the driver's seat.

As Vodka closed the gate, Sudan hauled a gidgee pole from the trailer and slid it onto the gate so that the end decorated with a red rag stuck out over the top.

He was giggling like a grizzled boy as he ran back to the tractor, Vodka following.

Their dust was still billowing over the gate when Boondoo set Lubra to jump it. She saw the red rag and reared. Boondoo fell and lay breathless, a roaring in his ears, and Des Parkes screaming, 'Listen, there's no way in the world you can win the Cup. No way you can enter. No way you can even get there.'

Boondoo grabbed for the rein that was hanging next to his face, pulled himself to his knees and fell again as his stock whip slipped from the snaffle ring.

He lay there and tasted the dust that his people said was Koonapipi, the earth mother. More slowly this time, he got to his feet and staggered towards the gate, leading Lubra while the cicadas sawed the day into burning seconds.

He heaved the gidgee pole from the gate, opened it and led Lubra through. He readjusted his improvised rein and remounted.

The tractor and trailer and Sudan and Vodka were dust hanging over the giant termite tower which marked the fourth gate.

Boondoo urged Lubra forward. She responded, her stride lengthening, the thud of her hoofs sending cattle in the track-side paddocks running from the shade they had found for themselves under the dusty gums.

34

Webster held the four-wheel drive steady as he turned off the black hiss of the bitumen onto the first corrugations of the track that curved north to Rainbow.

'That's where it started,' said Halliday.

'Don't follow,' said Tim Webster.

'Thinking,' said Halliday. He looked out of the window at the tawny paddocks roaring by. Of Italy. And the sun shining on the old cart track through the hills that was to have got him in front of the Allied spearhead.

'Goddamn desk jockeys,' said Halliday.

'Yeah.' Tim Webster bounced high in his seat as he failed to avoid a pothole. 'There's a lot of them about.'

'Goddamn desk jockeys were going to bust me.'

Ashby plugged a microphone lead into his tape recorder and moved from his seat to crouch, microphone extended, behind Halliday.

'After Anzio, right?' said Ashby. 'The military were threatening to take away your war correspondent's accreditation because you had linked with partisans, were leading a group.'

'Alaska, Fisi. The partisans were Eskimos fighting to protect their blubber from scented-soap fanciers.' He pushed Ashby's microphone away. 'And get your goddamn mike out of my ear before I shove it where you can record your inmost feelings.'

Ashby wedged the microphone in the pocket beside Halliday's seat and retreated to his own seat holding the tape recorder.

Halliday stared ahead at the track. Eskimos every one of them. Mario, Raff, Giuseppe on the old cart track through the hills that was to have got him in front of the spearhead. First to file from Rome, his lead all ready in his head. But-but-but. An abandoned supply truck and a skidding pause for the loot which refreshes.

Raff'd been trundling a big Parmesan cheese, using a long-necked wine flask.

But-but-but. The Kraut machine gun opened up, blowing the middle out of the cheese and slicing Raff in two.

'Kraut version of steak *cacciatore*,' said Halliday. 'You would've loved it, Fisi.'

Ashby unclipped his water bottle and moved forward to offer it to Halliday. 'Drink?'

'Not now,' said Halliday. And not then. Wine flask unbroken. No shortage of red as the machine gun, but-but-but, found Mario and Giuseppe where they were returning fire from under the supply truck and nailed them to the earth they'd dreamt of being given.

Their death screams brought silence. And strangest sound in war. Enemy talking, voices high with the excitement of killing. Knew what they were doing, those Krauts. Raff had been driving.

'One terrific driver,' said Halliday. '*Mille miglia* calibre. No nerves.'

Tim Webster, battling the corrugations of the track, grunted. Couldn't stand blokes peeing in his pocket.

Halliday gripped his rifle between his knees. Sue Cornwall, who had ignored his talk, couldn't ignore his trembling. 'Are you all right?' she said.

He nodded. Oh, terrific. Time he got into the driver's seat, the Krauts were having themselves some fun, bracketing the jeep with a mortar. Missed him with their third because he went into reverse. And their fourth. Got him with their fifth when he stalled on Raff's body, going forward.

'I watched from the top of St Peter's as the spearhead of the Allied forces moved in on Rome,' said Halliday.

'But you were wounded,' said Ashby.

'Best goddamn lead I never filed,' said Halliday.

His hand crept inside his safari jacket. The gold ring was there, hanging on a bootlace. Set in the ring, he could feel the jagged mortar fragment, one of six the sawbones'd cut out of him.

'That's where it did start,' said Halliday.

Tim Webster glanced across Sue Cornwall at him. Might be the sun. Have to get him to wear a hat. Finding one big enough could be a problem. He would have to be the 20-gallon size. At least.

114

Halliday pressed his thumb against the jagged mortar fragment. That was where the fear had started. And the fear had then started his body cells running amok.

35

Boondoo spat, trying to get rid of the taste of the dust as he leant from the saddle to close the fourth gate behind him.

The taste of the dust was defeat but Lubra was impatient to gallop. Boondoo rode her into a dip where in the Wet a creek ran. She got a whiff of the dried up carcase of a steer entangled in the branches of a tree where it had been swept by the last flood. He had to force her forward. Once past the carcase, Lubra told him he could catch Sudan and Vodka. The taste of the dust told him he could not. And the can of beer winking at him, frosted, from the top of a boulder told him to stop. He was ready to rein in when he realised that Sudan and Vodka must have stopped to leave the can of beer. He urged Lubra on between the fences that now lined the track on either side. Rounding a bend, he had a sight of Sudan and Vodka and the trailer and tractor.

Dust plumed behind them. Boondoo was eager to taste this dust.

On the tractor, Sudan shouted to Vodka, 'We're home and hosed and best of all the boong buys.' He concentrated on his driving, adding, 'All they're good for these days. Giving a man's tax back to him as booze.'

Vodka could see Boondoo coming on through the dust. 'I do not think he stopped for the beer.'

'Stop yabbering,' shouted Sudan. 'Stand by to put up another gidgee. Don't want the cunning bugger jumping the last gate.'

36

Ashby cavorted and crouched before Halliday clicking off shots as Halliday made a tour of the outside of the pub and its scatter of cabins.

'Oh, marvellous,' said Ashby when he got a shot of Halliday laughing at the way the cabins had been surrounded by low, boat-shaped trellis work so that they looked like little arks.

'Might just be by Disneyland out of Dachau,' said Halliday, twanging a strand of barbed wire.

'Do that again,' said Ashby.

Halliday glared at him. 'Wrap it round your throat, Fisi, you tell me to do anything again.'

Over by the four-wheel drive, Donaldson dumped his swag on the ground while Webster unbuckled the water bags from the front bull bar.

'Been looking for a bloke,' said Webster. 'Rouseabout. Bit of driving.'

Donaldson kicked his swag. 'Could do with somewhere to put this and some wages.'

'Couple of hundred is what I had in mind,' said Webster.

'A week?'

'Break it down. Fortnight. All found.'

Donaldson looked across at Sue Cornwall, who was taking a pair of sunglasses from her handbag. 'That include women?'

'Depends how they find you.'

'Never had a knock back in my life.'

'Keep trying. Happens to the unluckiest of us.' Webster held out the keys to the four-wheel drive. 'More interested in whether you can handle my vehicle.'

'If it's got wheels,' said Donaldson, taking the keys, 'I can drive it. If it hasn't, I can lift it.'

'Fair enough. Start with the luggage.'

Donaldson was listening but he was looking up at the top deck of the pub where Mary Parkes stood in her new apple-green cotton, her lips red and smiling with Lady Rose.

'Streuth,' whispered Donaldson, 'my old man used to talk about mutton dressed as lamb but I didn't know what the old bugger meant till now.'

Webster thumped him back-handed in the belly with the water bags. 'Your old man should've done that more often,' he growled, and shouted, 'Good to see you, Mary.'

'And you, Tim. You look funny without a mob.'

'Got a mob. Hope you're ready to yard them.'

'Plenty of room. Separate cabins for everyone as you said on the two-way.'

'Maybe a couple sharing.'

'Blokes?'

Webster shook his head. He introduced Sue Cornwall and then Donaldson as 'Sue' and 'Wayne'.

Sue Cornwall did not linger as Mary Parkes leapt to the wrong conclusion and Webster tried to set her right while confusing her further by introducing Halliday and Ashby.

The shade of the bar struck Sue Cornwall like blindness. She put on her sunglasses, conscious of shadows watching her. Another shadow floated above the bar, saying all in a rush, 'G'day. Des Parkes. You're a nice surprise.'

Gradually, she was able to make him out, a tubby, bald man wearing an old football guernsey. She lifted her sunglasses onto the top of her head. A blue guernsey with a big red V on it.

As she got him into focus, he moved sideways and round the bar to welcome Halliday who had his rifle cradled in the crook of his arm. She noticed that Halliday was again wearing the gold ring with the mortar fragment set in it that he had been wearing when they first met.

Against the wood of the rifle's stock, the gold gleamed when Ashby's camera flashed in the dimness.

Under his white hair, Halliday's face expected to be recognised. A new expression, that. Or had it once been confined to Caesars? And Cleopatras? Sue Cornwall smiled. She herself had felt the expression growing on her face. Another skin. Or a mould on cheese. Yes, a cheesey grin mould, grown from too many camera sessions and too many glances which wondered whether they could possibly have met her in bed.

Beauty Bubble was where they had met her. She was the Girl in the Beauty Bubble Bath. Every night is Beauty Bubble Bath Night. Except Book Bang Night when she had exploded from a giant cracker into the arms of Tembo Halliday. The great Tembo Halliday, honouring London with his presence and her with his attentions. Orchids, orchids, flowers of speech and their celebrity. That united them more than a vow, made them more noteworthy than a couple, made them an item.

She turned, her hair flaring in the dimness of the pub. Ogilvie was staring at her. He did not expect to be recognised, yet his face was unforgettable: a friendly threat, eyes set far back and dark under a ridge of brow, black hair hacked off, a nose which had taken a beating. And about him a great stillness.

Something else. Some other wound, pulsing in his stillness.

Sheean raised his beer can to her from its resting place on his paunch. She lowered her sunglasses and moved towards Halliday.

'Notice how she stared at me,' said Sheean. 'There's something about me.'

'Know that,' said Ogilvie.

'Beaut chick. Wonder what she's doing here.'

'She's no' selling the *War Cry*.'

'Doesn't have to. Not with everything else she's got to offer. Wasted on the old goat she's with.'

'Ach, don't be daft. He's her father.'

'He's old enough to be yours but he's not hers. And I'm ...' Sheean's voice tailed off. He hammered on the bar with his beer can. 'Another round. Another round. We're doing a perish here.'

Ogilvie took a sup of beer. 'Know what you are, Vin.'

Sheean kept hammering on the bar. 'You know nothing, you big Scots drongo. If she's his daughter, Jesus Christ's a lance corporal and I'm the voice crying in the wilderness. Make the rough ways shebeens, and the crooked ways speakeasies.' He raised his voice and chanted, 'Sherbert for the love of Allah. Sherbert.'

'Cut the kidding, Vin.'

'I'm not kidding. Lay you odds he won her knocking over clay pipes with that rifle of his. Makes a rusty musket of yours.'

Ogilvie crushed his beer can and gave it to Sheean. 'Put that in your gub and give it a chew.'

As Ogilvie strode to the door, Halliday put his arm round Sue Cornwall's shoulders. Sheean watched him. Old goat. Chick needed a young goat. A damned young goat.

'Any chance of a lift up the track?' he shouted to Halliday.

'Depends where you're headed,' Halliday said.

'Up the track.'

Ogilvie halted and rushed at Sheean, grabbing him by the throat. 'You're going nowhere.'

'Up –' said Sheean.

'Nowhere,' said Ogilvie and gave his mate a shake for further emphasis. He made for the door again, only to be blocked by Tim Webster, who offered him a drink.

'Not the now,' said Ogilvie, pushing past him and out into the sun.

119

Webster went after him. 'No hard feelings, Og.'

Ogilvie kept going. 'None,' he said.

'Later then,' said Webster and went into the bar.

The sun magicked a swirling willy-willy from hot air and dust which danced ahead of Ogilvie.

Good boss, the old Tim. No fuss. 'Nice day for travelling' was all he'd said. No bother. No sign he'd prevented a killing the day before.

Ogilvie rubbed his nose and doubled under the sun as he had doubled away from Tim Webster's safari camp to cut out his cheque and try to drown the past in whiskies and beers.

No drowning his mucker, Rodd, strapped stiff and silent in the asylum, staring a last message, 'Get me out of here. Get me home.'

No drowning Rodd. Nor McAskill.

Ogilvie punched the air as he doubled under the sun. Shouldn't've grabbed Vin by the throat, though. Never done it before. Wrong. Very wrong. Wasn't really Vin he'd wanted to grab. It was the big, white-haired bloke Vin'd said was old enough to be his father. It was his father he wanted to grab for scarpering and leaving his mother and him. Her to the grave. Him to the Institute, the Regiment, McAskill and worse.

37

Boondoo galloped Lubra to the top of the rise and reined in to give her a spell. Below he could see the track dipping and curving round an earth dam to the fifth gate. Beyond was the pub, wallowing drunkenly in the waves of heat.

At the fifth gate Sudan was putting up the last of three gidgee poles. Vodka was already running for the tractor. Boondoo leant forward to touch the scar on Lubra's neck, around which salty sweat had gathered, a third eye. Stupid. Stupid of him to let Sudan talk him into a race. By the time he cleared the gidgee poles, Sudan and Vodka would be in the pub.

The tractor growled away. Boondoo licked his fingers to get the salt from Boondoo's neck. Then, as lightly as if he were polishing his boot heels, he rubbed them on Lubra's flanks.

Down the slope they charged with Boondoo angling her to the offside of the track, his tongue click-clicking a faster, faster rhythm for her hoofs.

Where the track began to curve round the dam, Boondoo set Lubra at the nearside fence. Up, up and over she went with a crow cawing at the invasion of its sky. Boondoo gathered Lubra on the narrow flat between the fence and the earth wall of the dam, turning her simultaneously left-handed to go round the dam, out onto the wider flat beyond the fifth gate.

The going was easier in the paddock than on the track. Boondoo galloped Lubra for a good 500 yards until he got a sight of Sudan and Vodka pulling the tractor and trailer up in front of the pub.

Only then did he set Lubra at the fence again. She rose to it and was over but stumbling. Boondoo shifted his weight, lifting her in a scrabble of flying stones as Sudan cut the tractor engine.

In the silence, the clatter of Lubra's hoofs and the jingle and creak of her harness alerted Sudan. He took one look and leapt from the tractor seat, heading for the pub no more than thirty paces away.

Boondoo, low in the saddle, click–click-clicking, went after Sudan as though Sudan were an old bull, bound for the scrub. Lubra responded, galloping past Sudan and up the drumming gangplank into the hot shade of the pub.

Sue Cornwall screamed and Halliday yelled 'Eee-yah' at the sight of Boondoo, a fifth horseman from a new apocalypse – white jockey cap, bright green shirt, white britches, long boots and a big neckerchief, all frozen in memory by the flash of Ashby's camera.

Boondoo slid from Lubra's back, got hold of her bridle and calmed her, breathing into her nostrils. He tugged his stock whip from the snaffle ring and cracked it to greet Sudan when he rushed in followed by Vodka.

'Eee-yah,' Halliday yelled again. Even as he did he was conscious that Des Parkes, Vin Sheean and Tim Webster were being studiedly impassive as if a horse in a bar were as common as the cat on the mat. Should've remembered. Reaction of Australians was not to react. He'd noticed it in 'Nam. He took out his tape recorder, switched it on and said, 'F is for face. Question. Are Australians Asian in maintaining impassivity? Or is national face affected by convict need not to betray emotion?'

Des Parkes and Tim Webster exchanged looks. Sheean said to Webster, 'Your mate beats listening to the women magging away on the two-way radio.'

'Right,' said Webster. 'What about a beer?'

'Mine,' said Halliday.

'I buy', said Vodka.

Sudan ducked under Lubra's head to get to the bar. 'You haven't got any money, you reffo bastard.' He noticed Sue Cornwall. 'Jeez, a sheila. Didn't see you there at first. Come to help with the cooking, I hope. No offence, Des, but your Mary's stew would cause a riot in an Army mess.'

Vodka slapped Boondoo on the back. 'You ride like lancer. Nothing is stopping you. Not the gidgee poles. Not the fences.'

Sudan broke off from introducing himself. 'Fences. You're nuts on fences. When I was a kid, I didn't know what a fence was. Never worked fenced country. First wire I ever saw from a horse was Johnny Turk's. My oath it was. Johnny Turk's wire at Bersheeba.'

'Underage,' said Halliday, 'betcha.'

Sudan looked at Tim Webster. 'You might introduce a bloke.'

When Webster did, Sudan said, 'Too bloody right I was underage. And underweight. Lightest light horsemen at Bersheeba. The horse was too stupid to be scared and I was too young to know better.'

'Missed first round of world-title bout,' said Halliday. 'Saw your boys in second –'

'If you mean the Second World War. Was in it, too.'

'Have a drink.'

'Kokoda Track,' said Sudan, 'Up was a bastard. Down was a cow.'

'Have a drink,' Halliday repeated.

Vodka took his hand and shook it. 'Mahonsky. They call me Vodka. But my mate Sudan is buying. We have bet with Boondoo.'

Des Parkes hammered on the bar with his wooden mallet. 'No one buys a drink for that cheeky boong.'

'Bucket for the horse then,' yelled Halliday, spreading his roll of dollars along the bar. 'Bucket for the horse.'

They all took up the yell. Lubra whinnied.

Sudan said, 'Bucket of beer.'

They all yelled, 'Bucket of beer. Bucket of beer.'

Parkes got a green plastic bucket, placed it on the bar and began to range cans alongside it. As fast he put them up, Sudan or Vodka or Sheean opened them and poured them into the bucket till it was foaming full.

Sheean placed his hands on either side of the bucket. He raised it from the bar, turning as he did so. Ashby's camera flashed. Lubra shied. Sheean bowed to the horse and began to drink the bucket of beer himself. At first there were protests. Then it became clear what he intended. Silence fell as the others counted his Adam's apple registering his gulps.

Sudan picked up the count. 'Five, six, seven, eight, nine, ten, eleven, twelve . . .'

At twenty, Sheean fell to his knees, still drinking. At thirty, he belched back into the bucket. Des Parkes said, 'Chunder in here and you're barred.'

Sheean kept drinking. At forty-five, he was sitting back on his heels. At ninety, he drained the last of the beer and his face was the colour of the bucket.

He stretched out flat on his back, belched once, twice, rolled over on his face and lay quiet.

Vodka returned the bucket to Des Parkes. 'Sudan's shout now,' he said. 'Boondoo?'

'Water,' said Boondoo, 'for me and my horse.'

'Mine. Mine, you black bastard. The horse is mine,' Parkes shouted. 'And the other one. I bought them fair and square.'

'Can't see your problem,' said Halliday. 'You bought them, you must have paper.'

'Had. Had. But I don't know where it's got to. That big Scots bastard Ogilvie stuck his bib in. The paper's vanished.'

Sheean stirred. 'Call him a bastard to his face in that tone of voice and I'll have to clean you off the floor.'

Raging, Parkes came round the end of the bar. He kicked Sheean in the side. 'Where's that paper?' Sheean did not move. 'Give you a hint,' he said. And farted.

Parkes kicked him again. 'Ratbag. There's a lady here.'

'Not my lady. Not your lady,' Sheean said. 'Our lady of Rainbow.'

'Bloody ratbag. Lying there. You should see yourself.'

'Do.'

Saw himself lonely, stretched out on marble, knowing he would not be able to withdraw at the last moment as he had told himself he would to get himself that far.

Story of his life. Bel was right. Plurry wanker. He rolled over so that he was facing the floor and stretched his arms out on either side of him. *Tu es wanker in aeternum secundum ordinem Onan.* Thou art a wanker for ever according to the order of Onan.

Parkes turned on Boondoo. 'The paper. I want to know where it is.' He reached for the horse's bridle. 'And until I do, she's mine.'

Lubra reared up. Sudan said, 'She doesn't think so.' And Vodka added, 'A bet's a bet. It is my mate's shout. Water for Boondoo and his horse. For me the usual and a beer for my mate, Sudan.'

'I'll order for myself, you mug reffo.'

'Your English not so good,' said Vodka, 'when it comes to your shout.'

Boondoo was already leading Lubra to the door, when Parkes yelled, 'Don't come back.' And to Vodka and Sudan, 'No booze till you off-load the trailer. I don't want the beer bloody boiled.'

'Right, boss,' said Sudan, making for the door. Vodka followed.

On the floor, Sheean began to sing. He sang, 'Gentleman wanker off on a spree. Doomed from here to Eternity.'

Des Parkes roared, 'Shut up, you ratbag. I told you there's a lady present.'

Sheean laughed. 'Present her then,' he said, 'and I might be able to serve her.'

'You haven't got what it takes,' said Halliday. And to Sue Cornwall, 'Right, Bibi?'

'You would know,' she said, 'who better?'

38

Ogilvie pulled the rawhide rope tighter on the bundles of brush-wood, pressing them closer against the corrugated iron of the roof which burnt his hand.

He took a sup of water from the canvas water bag lying on the roof beside him, rinsed the water round in his mouth and squirted it out on his hand. He looked down at Bel, who was helping him.

'I'm wondering whether this brushwood'll catch fire. The roof here's hotter than the lid of hell.'

Bel climbed the ladder to pass him a lump of concrete. 'You catch fire maybe. You going too fast.'

'Want to finish this last roof.' He eased himself towards the roof ridge and sat astride to adjust the rawhide ropes.

He wiped his face with the old Balmoral, staring towards the river where Bel's kids were playing, guarded by Bobbie, pelting him and each other with mud, shrieking and laughing. Their laughter came to him faintly as from the past and there was no pain in their shrieks. He knew why and he was going to say why when Bel cut in on his thought.

'Smoko time.'

'Got to finish this last roof first.'

They worked in silence until the roof was completely covered with brushwood and tied down with weighted rawhide.

Bel had the billycan with a spout on the camp fire. She poured two mugs full of tea. She and Ogilvie went into the two-room house, the roof of which they had finished covering with brush-wood. Ogilvie said, 'Cooler, eh?'

Bel blew on her tea. 'Not very big.'

'Ach, don't let them con you, Bel. They want you to think that. They want you to think you haven't got a prayer here with all your kids. They want you to think that because they hope to hell it's true. They hope these wee places'll scare the life out of you. Aye, and all the others like you. They want to scare the life out of you so's they don't have to change their own lives.' Ogilvie rubbed the hot mug of tea along the bruiselike mark on his forearm. Rodd. His mucker Rodd had said something similar. 'They think if they put people in wee houses, the people will think they have minds to match.'

Bel took this in with her tea, watching Ogilvie over the rim of her mug as he talked. 'You sick?' she asked.

'I'm OK,' he said, 'and so will you be. I mean, they're no' palaces but you've got the four of them to spread yourself around in.'

'That cop, the new walloper in Yelboom, he's not going to like it, he come this way.'

'Let him lump it. Tell him you're a squatter and what was empty you made your own. And if he gets angry give him a wee mirror so's he can look at himself.'

The heavy darkness of Bel's face lightened in a smile. She went outside. Ogilvie stayed where he was, supping his tea. Some woman, Bel. He paced the length of the empty house. She must need more beds. The spare stretchers from the Bachelor Quarters would never be missed. He rattled his empty mug across the corrugated-iron wall of the house and with a drum roll sounding in his mind went out to rejoin Bel who was sitting by the camp fire.

'That Vin,' she said, 'he's not going to marry into me properly.'

'It's the way he is.'

'Don't want him anyway no more. Silly wanker. All that monkey yabber.'

'You've lost me.'

Bel put down her mug of tea. 'When that Vin asleep.' She beat her breast with her clenched fist. 'Punch himself allersame Tarzan and all the time that monkey yabber.'

Now Ogilvie knew what she meant. He'd heard Vin at the monkey yabber, surprised. No mistaking it. He had heard it first with Rodd, his mucker, for whom he had lost three stripes. Aye, in Jerusalem.

'To hell the stripes,' he said. 'What about me?'

'You be all right by and by.'

Ogilvie closed his eyes and nodded. He would and all, now he had Vin. And Vin's monkey yabber. Wise monkey. True yabber.

Bel lifted the billycan from the edge of the fire. 'More tea. You real crook. Must be.' She made a face to imitate his, a face of pain.

'I'm OK, I tell you.'

Ogilvie saw how Bel seemed to grow from the shadowed earth where she sat.

Years of love which must find its way, or for ever sour to hatred, swept over him. He embraced Bel, holding Bel as he had always promised himself he would hold his mother who had surely held him once. Otherwise, how could he have lived?

'You good,' said Bel, 'mighty.'

'Not me,' said Ogilvie, 'you. I wanted to tell you up on the roof. Listen to your kids. You're why they're not afraid. You're why they're happy.'

Ogilvie stepped out of the house's shadow, taking some of it with him, taller than he was on the red dust. Rodd's shadow. McAskill's dust. And McAskill's rule for interrogation in the field: work from what you know to what you think the prisoner may know. It can be more effective and less messy than a blowtorch.

McAskill's rule'd been effective with Vin all right. Ogilvie doubled under the sun. The only monkey yabber he'd ever learned had given him the chance to double-check Vin's monkey yabber.

'Presbo comedian,' Vin'd said after he'd got a few drinks in him. 'You sound as if you're gargling iron filings. But if you're saying *Vincere aut Perdere Omnia*, it's Latin for To Win or Lose it All – the last line of your drunk's recitation, you dill.'

39

Des Parkes opened another can of beer and put it, hissing, on the bar where Halliday's finger indicated it should go, amid the array of cans he had already gathered in front of him. Halliday said, 'Australia's last gasp will come from a can of bull.'

'American bull,' said Sue Cornwall, 'stamped all over with the presidential seal of withdrawal.'

Halliday smiled at her, his lips seemingly pasted flat to his teeth. 'Always willing to defer to a cow on the subject of bull.'

Ashby's camera flashed on Sue Cornwall. Tim Webster clutched his own throat and made choking noises. Parkes passed him an unopened can of beer and said to Sue Cornwall, 'The missus usually has tea about now. She'd be pleased for you to join her, I'm sure.'

Halliday said, 'Bibi would rather have V and V.'

'Vodka and something?' said Des Parkes.

'No. Vitriol and vinegar. Intravenous.'

'Vodka will do,' said Sue Cornwall. 'With tonic and a slice of lemon.'

Sheean laughed.

Halliday said, 'You're Vodka, right?'

'No, Vodka's outside.' Sheean emptied his can, put it down next to Halliday's array and picked up a full one. 'I'm beer.'

'Noticed that.' Halliday chuckled. 'Your *companero*. Big guy in crazy hat sure gave you fond farewell.'

'He has his mad moments,' said Sheean heading for the door. 'But I wouldn't call his hat crazy.'

'Mean kind of a big guy,' Halliday said to Webster. 'Seemed to know you too.'

'Everyone knows everyone up here. A man'll drive hundred miles out of his way to talk to a bloke he doesn't much care about to stop himself talking to himself.'

Halliday waved his can from side to side in front of Webster's face. 'Tim, Tim. Old street reporter Halliday. Asks question. Expects answer. Knows evasion. Repeats question.'

'Worked for me,' said Webster, 'Name's Ogilvie. Alec.'

'Booze. Betcha.'

'Takes his share. Have to up here or you end up dry as a mummy's ...' Webster glanced sideways at Sue Cornwall. 'Sorry.'

Halliday said, 'Yeah, mummy's sorry can be very dry.'

'What I meant was, it wasn't only booze with Ogilvie. He's cheeky with it. Way a boong's cheeky. Got nothing. Never will have. Gives you a look and you're down and he's a winner.'

'Know what you mean,' said Halliday, taking a drink. But he saw this Ogilvie differently from the way Tim did. Ogilvie had soldier written all over him. Walk, eyes, the shave so close the jawline gleamed. Not cheeky. Undefeated.

Webster finished his beer. 'I didn't mind the cheekiness so much but when Og started on a client.'

Halliday put his arm round Sue Cornwall's shoulders. 'Woman client. Betcha.'

Ashby's camera flashed in the dimness. Webster took the can of beer Des Parkes handed to him. 'Ducks,' he said. 'Started with ducks. Ogilvie was in charge of one of my outcamps. I got there with the client. A Pom and –'

'This Pom bit,' said Halliday, 'been asking about it since arrival. Nobody knows. Correction, everybody knows but they give you different answer. Short for pomegranate, one guy says, because English have red faces. Another guy says corruption of Prisoner Of Mother England. Another, Jimmy Grant, rhyming slang for immigrant, rhyming slang for pomegrant, mispronunciation of pomegranate, brings us back to Pom. American calls Englishman Limey, he knows why. Lime juice. But Pom.'

'A Pom is a Pom is a Pom,' said Webster.

Ashby's camera flashed. 'Same as a rose.'

Sheean re-entered the bar. 'But Poms don't usually smell as sweet as roses,' he said. 'Heard about a Pom once. Left a bath to his wife. It was still in its packing case and when she opened it, she

130

didn't know what it was for. Tried to roast a pig in it. Tasted terrible. She forgot to take the pig's uniform off.'

'Is he for real?' Halliday said to Webster.

'Of course I am,' said Sheean. 'I've read your book *Deadline Rome, Dateline Death*. Very accurate.'

Halliday snapped his fingers. Des Parkes opened a can of beer for him. Halliday passed it to Sheean. 'You knew Rome during second round, world-title bout?'

Ashby said, 'Tembo means World War Two. He was at ringside.'

'I know what I mean,' said Halliday. 'And I know where I was. So does this guy.'

Sheean nodded and gulped the beer. He knew Rome twice over. In the war against sin when he was invisible in black. In the flight from the Faith, when he returned to Rome all shining with God's loot to see himself reflected in the eyes of its women.

'You didn't answer question,' said Halliday.

'I've got an instinct for the truth I've got to avoid.'

'Funny guy.'

'Very.' Sheean peered into the beer can. Vin the Visigoth from Down Under. Only guy in history to paint Rome, the Scarlet Woman, red with her own gold. Should've stayed. Not lobbed back to Oz with his scrotum full of memories and his pockets full of nothing.

'Aw, look,' said Tim Webster.

'I am looking,' said Sheean.

'What I meant is, where was I?'

'Your outcamp,' said Ashby.

'Yeah, well, you know what Poms are.' Webster drank from the can, his little finger delicately extended and decorated with the ring pull from the can and all the others he had drunk. 'Very correct, Poms. And there was Ogilvie blasting off at a mob of sitting ducks. Client wasn't impressed.'

131

'Not impressed myself,' said Halliday. 'Nothing sweeter than wing-shot on duck.'

'Ogilvie didn't see it that way. He was shooting for some boongs camped by the lagoon. Dropped the client.' Webster hooked the air with his fist.

Halliday said, 'Punched him out?'

'Started with a punch. But the client got up and it was on like one thing.' Webster made a chopping motion with his hand. 'The client could use himself and so can Ogilvie. Pommie.'

'The client?' said Halliday. 'The client?'

'McAskill. Kenneth McAskill.'

Old street reporter Halliday gave no sign of recognition.

Webster continued, 'Pommie officer. No error. Saw a few when I was in North Africa. Half the length of their little swagger canes and twice as snappy. I expected him to press charges against Ogilvie. Not a murmur.'

'Scared,' said Halliday.

'Not McAskill. No, the thing was I got the impression he and Ogilvie knew each other from somewhere. Anyway, the client first. I had to thump Ogilvie to stop him. Piece of ironwood. Thick skull, Ogilvie. No wonder he gets on so well with the boongs.'

The pub creaked in the heat as if it were once more on the river. Sheean put the cold can to his head. Og hadn't told him about the fight. Or about Tim Webster having to thump him. That was it. The thumping had knocked Og's brains adrift.

Halliday said, 'I suppose the big guy speaks their lingo, the boongs'.'

'Their bottle talk. When he really gets on the turps, only a boong would give him houseroom.'

'He initiated?'

'In the way of the flagon.' Webster sucked on his can of beer, then pretended to spew. 'And the chunder.'

Halliday laughed. 'Be interested to see an initiation ceremony or one of their corroborees.'

'No chance. Not here anyway. Might get something set for you further in. Around here, well, let's face it, the poor bastards have as much to corroboree about as battery hens have to cackle.'

'Ones I've seen so far sure wouldn't make spare ribs at a Ku Klux Klan barbecue.'

Sue Cornwall released herself from Halliday's embrace and moved to the far end of the bar.

'Here,' said Halliday.

'You don't own me.'

'Didn't say that, Bibi.' Halliday took a wad of dollar bills from his pocket and folded them into a tube lengthways. 'But you do have a weakness for Uncle Sam's folding aphrodisiac.' He thrust the roll of notes towards her. Webster and Parkes exchanged looks. Parkes put four more cans of beer on the bar.

Halliday swung round to Ashby. 'Help with drinks. You're standing there like Billy Graham trying to look flattered as the monks brew him up a run of Southern Baptist Chartreuse.'

Ashby headed for the door. 'The tapes. Must transcribe them.'

'Tapes.' Halliday laid the roll of notes on the bar. 'Life's for living.'

Sue Cornwall said, 'The mama bear, the papa bear and the baby bear. They're not doing much living. Or the zoo full of other animals you've shot. Now it's sheep. I used to wonder about you and this.' She picked up Halliday's rifle. 'I don't any more.'

She threw the rifle at him. Halliday caught it and said, 'Keep your Freud dry.'

She lifted the bar flap and went behind the bar where another door led off to the rest of the pub and the cabins.

'Here,' Halliday shouted. The pain was back. It had come with her. He should give it back to her. He brought the rifle to his shoulder and pinned her in the crosshairs. Fly in a web. He fired. A bottle of cherry syrup shattered on a shelf above and behind Sue Cornwall and exploded onto her screaming head.

'Would've been your brains,' said Halliday, 'if I'd thought you had any.'

Still screaming, Sue Cornwall ran out.

'Fair go,' said Des Parkes. 'This is a pub. Not a shooting gallery.'

Webster took one of the cans from the bar and opened it, putting the ring pull on his pinkie with the ones already there. 'Guns and women don't mix. Like rum and whisky.'

The spent case tinkled on the floor as Halliday said, 'Need her.'

'Not you,' said Webster. 'Where we're headed, there's any number of women who'll climb into your swag at starshine and leave at sparrowfart.' He laughed on a swallow of beer and coughed. 'Can't even see them in the dark but, jeez, you know they're there.'

Halliday shook his head and pushed the roll of notes towards Des Parkes. 'Take the damage out of Uncle Sam's cock.'

Parkes picked up the roll of notes. He tried to moisten his thumb on his tongue. But his tongue was the drier. He began to count. Sheean counted with him. And faster, faster. 'Thirty-five thousand, six hundred and nineteen,' he said.

'God's sake,' said Parkes, keeping his thumb moving, 'have another beer and shut up.' And, before Sheean could speak again, 'I mean shut up and have another beer. No, I mean –' His thumb stopped moving and he roared, 'Bastard, you made me lose the bloody count.'

'Don't worry,' said Sheean, 'the countess will find him.'

'Out,' Des Parkes roared. 'Out.'

Halliday said, 'Nine hundred and fifty.' He leant his rifle in the angle of the wall and the bar. 'Tell me when it's finished. Plenty more where it came from.'

'Fort Knox,' said Sheean.

'The Soviet Union,' said Halliday. 'Went there earlier this year. Had a whole heap of frozen royalties to collect. The Commies wouldn't let me take my roubles out. Changed roubles into ikons. Brought ikons out. Sold ikons at profit. Like taking candy from a kid. Except the Commies think those kind of candies are mind rot.'

'Did something similar myself once,' said Sheean, 'years ago.'

'And made thirty-five thousand, six hundred and nineteen dollars. Betcha.'

'No bet.' Sheean leant over the bar to get a dripping cleaning cloth from the sink. 'Strictly a steal.' He wiped his face and hands with the cloth and went to the end of the bar to clean up the cherry syrup.

A blowfly was caught in the cherry syrup. Very carefully Sheean lifted the blowfly and placed it clear of the syrup. A column of ants, making for the syrup, found the blowfly and began to dismember it.

Sheean got down on his knees to wipe up the syrup, leaving the blowfly to the ants. If he hadn't played God, the blowfly would've died happily in syrup before the ants got to it. There was a sermon somewhere in that.

40

Mary Parkes insisted on giving Wayne Donaldson the grand tour of the pub's upper deck after he carried the luggage to the various cabins. He didn't mind too much. It gave him a chance to work out what he wanted to say and tell her.

Now he watched as she sat down in front of the transceiver which shared a mahogany side table in what had been the upper saloon with her collection of scent bottles and a series of white doilies embroidered with the signatures of visitors.

135

She clicked the transceiver on for sending and gave her call sign, Delta Hotel Lima Seven.

All along the radio arteries, men and women paused to listen as she repeated, 'This is Delta Hotel Lima Seven. Delta Hotel Lima Seven. Urgent. Do you read me?'

From the radio base, a thousand miles east, Dimity Milson responded, her English accent unmistakable, 'Not the other one, Mary love, I hope. Over.'

Mary Parkes's hand strayed to where her breast had been. Cheeky Pommie bitch. Mentioning that. Calling her 'love'. She bent to the transceiver microphone. 'This is Mrs Desmond Parkes at the Rainbow Hotel–Motel. Over.'

'Know that, Mary love. But I'm not doing the social pages today. Your urgent message, please. Is it medical? Over.'

'Telegram for Pan Australia Finance – P for penny, A for ackers, F for franc – Pan Australia Finance, Collins Street, Melbourne. Telegraphic address, Panaustral. Over.'

'Go ahead, Mary love.'

Mary Parkes mouthed the word 'Pommie' to Wayne Donaldson before speaking into the microphone again. 'Telegram reads: "Reference your letter about repossession of prime mover license CBY – C for Charlie, B for Barcoo, Y for Yagoona – 623 and ancillary equipment unless immediate payment eleven thousand two hundred and nine dollars and sixty-five cents stop". Got that? Over.'

'Roger, Mary love. Very sad. Over.'

'Telegram continues: "This vehicle is now lying by the Rainbow Track thirty-five miles south of Midnight Creek stop. Please repossess at your convenience and oblige Wayne Donaldson." Over.'

Dimity Milson's voice rose from its monotone. 'You beauty. Oh, you beauty, Mary love. Over.'

'Not my telegram. Mr Donaldson's. Wayne Donaldson. Owner

of the vehicle. He travelled up the track with Tim Webster who was accompanied by Tembo Halliday, the writer who's staying over here with his colleague Lewis Ashby and Sue Cornwall, a friend. Over.'

'Friend of Mr Ashby's, Sue Cornwall? Over?'

'No, of Tembo Halliday. Over.'

'You have all the fun, Mary love. Over.'

Mary Parkes clicked off the send switch. Donaldson took out his wallet. Mary Parkes shook her head. 'Later. When you've got yourself sorted out.'

Donaldson was already at the door. 'Thanks,' he said, and tripped over the combing in his haste. 'Thanks a lot.'

'Some tea?' said Mary Parkes.

'No,' said Donaldson.

He knew what he wanted. He wanted the tall, freckled chick.

41

Des Parkes crept round from the back of the pub and spoke to Sudan and Vodka in a whisper that had the force of a shout. 'You blokes mad? I told you to off-load the grog.'

They were sprawled in the shade of the trailer drinking beer.

Sudan said, 'We are off-loading it.'

'Into the cold room, I meant,' Parkes whispered, 'not into your flaming guts.'

'Same as your granddad when you get angry,' said Sudan. 'Sit down and have a beer.'

'Get that grog off-loaded. She must be boiling.'

Sudan took a mouthful of beer and rolled it round in his mouth. 'She's right.' He held out the can. 'Taste it yourself.'

'Get that grog off-loaded, I said.'

'You didn't say whether you wanted it through the front door or the back.'

'The back, of course.'

'Tractor won't start.'

'The front then. I don't care.'

'Not running short, are you?'

'That's not the point. I've got Tembo Halliday inside.'

'Not a bad cut of a bloke,' said Sudan, 'for a Yank.'

Des Parkes began to let down the tailgate of the trailer. 'But what's he going to think of a pub where the boss can't get his grog off-loaded? What's he going to write?'

'No worries. Man who has to write things down has nothing worth listening to.'

'What about a man who can hardly write his own name, you old bastard?'

'There's none better. If he's me, he's the ringer. First to lead them and head them. If he's your granddad.' Sudan threw his empty can across the track. 'Don't have to tell you about your own granddad, do I?'

Vodka's chest heaved in silent laughter. He enjoyed such conversations, wondering what a commissar would make of them. He went to the trailer and lifted a carton of beer under either arm.

'Bloody reffos,' said Sudan. 'Born with a whip cracking in their ear.'

Des Parkes followed Vodka up the gangplank carrying a single carton of beer.

Sudan groaned and stood up. At the trailer, he stacked three cartons of beer one on top of the other and staggered up the gangplank into the pub.

138

42

Sue Cornwall washed the cherry syrup out of her hair and stood in the shower booth enjoying the fall of water on her body and the play of broken sunlight shining through the bottles from which the booth was built. Other shower booths also built of empty bottles – whisky, brandy, sherry, beer and port – set in cement were arranged round a corrugated-iron tank set on stilts into which borewater was pumped to be gravity-fed to the showers.

The water from Sue Cornwall's shower ran in a concrete channel to fan out into the furrows of a vegetable patch where lettuce, potatoes, carrots and beans flourished and the bare toes of Wayne Donaldson wriggled. He pulled a carrot up, rubbed it clean on his shorts and began to chew.

Sue Cornwall could not get the soap to lather. It slid over her body as if both were marble, making her feel more than ever a shell wrapped round a shy otherness. She rubbed the soap under her arms, remembering suddenly: 'Strange little thing' and 'But pretty'. Her mother and father discussing their changeling. From the time of those remarks, she had accentuated the prettiness to hide the strangeness, the sense of space between herself and the body she could not quite feel she filled.

At first she thought the hands reaching for her breasts from behind were Halliday's. Her hesitation confirmed Donaldson in his belief that she was the chick he had imagined winning from the Pom he had king-hit. She turned in his embrace and he swallowed her scream. Her nails raked at his face and her knee came up. She slipped and he had her down, the water beating against her face; her hair washing red towards the outlet as he tried to find her. He could not, and forced his tongue into her mouth to get a bearing on where he wanted to be. She bit his tongue and he growled in pain.

139

Her hand raked at his face again. His hand came up to fend her off and his blood rained down on her face, closing her eyes.

Her struggles grew more frantic, his more certain. There was a thud. 'Oh,' he moaned, 'Mum.'

She opened her eyes. Above her and astride Donaldson stood Ogilvie. He let the stone in his hand fall, splashing.

'You okay, woman?'

'Yes.'

His hand came down and patted her on the cheek. He rolled Donaldson off her and more of his blood went swirling round the stone to the vegetable patch. He gripped Donaldson's wrist, heaving him up on his shoulder as he backed out of the shower booth and into the past.

There had been a woman with the man. His wife. And a child. His son. McAskill had known the man might be able to resist coming to see her but could not resist coming to see his newborn son. Three weeks McAskill'd kept them watching the man's house in Belfast, shifting from laundry van to removal truck to midden motor.

The man'd come through the checkpoints as a British soldier, home on leave. Not without previous experience. All his papers in order and bags of swank although in civvies.

They'd given him enough time, as McAskill'd whispered to get a tension-easing laugh, to fuck himself silly and then had baled out of the midden motor and broken in so quickly that McAskill'd had what he called his popgun at the man's head before the man could get to the .45 under his pillow.

A mistake, that 7.65 at the man's head. He'd realised they'd come to lift him alive. He'd knocked the 7.65 up and fought them silently, one against a stick of four, trying not to wake his son in the cradle while his wife moaned her grief. Not for long.

She'd risen up in fury to help her man. McAskill'd trained them for every scenario. Except a naked woman, strong in fury, milk streaming from her breast at the whimpering of her child. For a moment they'd all been children again. And the man'd made it to the outside door when Yours Truly Alec Ogilvie, had belted him with the first thing to hand, an electric iron. The dull crack had roused the son fully to howl the roses off the wallpaper and the man to say, 'Wheesht, wee fella, wheesht.'

He had changed, the man, changed utterly. But when the hand-cuffs were snapped on him, he'd said, 'Still on provost duty then, Big Fella?' And was at once recognisable: Rodd, changed utterly but still cheeky with it in the way of the Regiment, 'Should've realised you were in that midden motor. I mean, what else would cowboys like you do low-level jump training for if not for jumping out of midden motors?'

Ogilvie began to double, trying to get away from the past. Donaldson came to, shifting on Ogilvie's shoulder. 'Sorry, pal,' said Ogilvie, still in the past as he put Donaldson down in the present shade of the empty water tank, 'Had to do it.'

'Thought.' Donaldson licked the blood from his lips and waved off the flies. 'Thought I knew her somehow.'

'Hoped,' said Ogilvie, 'as who wouldn't.'

'She all right.'

'Aye, but I don't think she really goes for you.'

'She wanted it. I know she did.' Donaldson got to his feet. 'What say we share her?' He put his hand in the pocket of his shorts. 'Toss you for first. Heads I crack her. Tails you -'

Ogilvie grabbed Donaldson by the upper arms and pulled him forward, his head gong to meet the bridge of Donaldson's nose. Donaldson slumped to the ground.

'You're lucky, pal,' said Ogilvie, 'you deserve this.' And touched Donaldson with the toe of his boot.

Donaldson gripped Ogilvie's ankle and tugged. Ogilvie went

down. He heard one of Bel's kids shout, 'A knuckle. A knuckle. A knuckle. It's a knuckle.'

Ogilvie stood up. Donaldson rushed him and drove him sprawling into the empty water tank. When Donaldson dived in on top of him, the water tank started to roll. Stones rattled against it as Bel's other kids took up the shout, 'A knuckle. A knuckle. It's knuckle.'

Donaldson's fist, in time with the rattling stones, beat against Ogilvie's face.

Kids'd stoned the ambulance when they'd taken Rodd away. They'd taken him out on a stretcher and his wife'd cried down curses, holding up Rodd's son as a witness. All along the street, dustbin lids'd clanged and the kids'd thrown stones at them.

The water tank rattled and bumped down the slope. Donaldson kept punching. Ogilvie took the punches, took them because of Rodd, his mucker, and the kids who'd shouted, 'Brits and shites. Out. Out.'

There was a final crash as the water tank hit the old car. Donaldson crawled out. Bel's kids drew back from him.

He ducked to shout into the water tank, his voice echoing. 'You coming out – or do I have to drag you out, you Pommie bastard?'

Ogilvie exploded from the water tank. Donaldson met his charge but could not hold it. Ogilvie spread-eagled him. The blade of Ogilvie's hand was up when the appeal in Donaldson's eyes halted the killing stroke.

Ogilvie hauled Donaldson to his feet. 'You make it?'

Donaldson shoved him away. 'I'll make you wish you'd never been born.'

'Wished that already, pal,' said Ogilvie and strode towards the Bachelor Quarters.

Sue Cornwall glimpsed Ogilvie as he passed her cabin and watched him from the window. As he neared the Bachelor Quarters, two boys came towards him, pulling a billy cart on which they had balanced upright the old dressmaker's dummy. Ogilvie gave them a salute and his voice carried to her. 'Hey, Eddie, Shane. Don't let Vin see you with his Matilda.' The boys laughed. 'Here a minute,' said Ogilvie, and Eddie and Shane followed him into the Bachelor Quarters. When they came out again, each was carrying a rolled-up stretcher which he loaded on the billy cart. Ogilvie did not come out again.

Sue Cornwall moved from the window and looked at herself in the dressing-table mirror, half expecting, half hoping to see a mark on her cheek where he'd touched her.

Nothing. She began to make up her face. But stopped, caught by the memory of the way he'd said, 'Woman.' 'You OK, woman?' She cleaned the make-up from her face. He had asked for nothing. And there had been no presumption, no complicity in his face. She stared at her naked reflection.

43

Halliday sketched a toast to everyone in the bar and drank nothing. He peered into his beer can. 'Women big cats. Most time blanks scare them. But when they go for your balls, it's live ammo time, boys.'

Parkes winked at Webster as Halliday's hand wavered over the array of beer cans in front of him.

'Catch the piggie by the toe,' Halliday said, and when Parkes kept winking, 'Should do something about that eye, Des. Knew a guy once. Couldn't control nervous tic. Eyelid fell off. Had to wear a black patch. Hanged for a pirate.'

Parkes put his hand over his eye. 'Only thinking we ought to award you an OBE.'

'That right?'

'Order of the Boozer Empire for services to the Australian brewing industry.'

'Sure is one good beer. Kind of a Budweiser with added pow.'

Halliday selected another can. Secret was getting drunk enough to short-circuit dull hunches and let wild ones spring. Needed stamina. He raised the can, again drinking nothing. Stamina and cunning and money. The hell with silence and exile. He pushed the empty can back among the array so that a full can was pushed further down the bar to where Sheean was. Stamina, cunning and money. And a sneaky saucehead under impression he was putting one over you by drinking your beer.

Halliday selected a half-full can. 'My first wife was big cat. Big lady pussy. *Une jolie laide*, they used to swear in Paris. Alackaday I ever laid her. She was more *laide* than *jolie*.'

Parkes put the dingo scalp on the bar. Halliday said, 'Been shooting pussy?'

'Dingo,' said Parkes. 'Not me but. The big Scots bloke. Trapped it and then shot it.'

Halliday took a careful gulp of beer. 'Kind of way is that for guy to hunt? Sitting ducks. Trapping dingos, then shooting them.' He slapped Webster on the back. 'You did good canning that big ...' His voice tailed off into a knowing grin.

Old street reporter Halliday wasn't always as drunk as he appeared. Old street reporter Halliday wasn't going to tell all he knew about McAskill and his merry men till he was good and goddamn ready.

Webster opened a fresh can of beer for Halliday and one for himself. Halliday rubbed the dingo scalp. 'Be nice to get one of these.'

'Guarantee it,' said Webster, placing the ring pull from his beer can on his pinkie with the others. 'Knew a sheila once who took scalps.'

'Don't they all?'

'This sheila was hawking her fork for scalps. Reckoned the bounty was more than she would have got in cash. Married she was and got herself up the duff by one of her clients.'

'Husband sure must've been happy about that.'

Webster grinned. 'Man's a cow to keep talking about a woman. But this sheila told her husband. And him in the bush most the time timber getting. She told him, "If you were cut with a circular saw, you wouldn't know which tooth it was."'

'So what happened?'

'The bastard lost her.'

'Died of the pox, I suppose.'

Webster laughed. 'Not her. He took her out into the bush and lost her. Walked her round in circles and left her.'

Halliday said, 'No name, I guess.'

Webster's hand rasped against his jaw and the collection of ring can pulls on his pinkie tinkled. 'May Brown. May Smith. May Leary.'

And Sheean said, 'May God forgive you, Tim. That story's got more whiskers on it than you have.'

Halliday picked up another of his cans. 'Folks in Adelaide gave me distinct impression Outback women were all pure, white and never done.'

Sheean staggered to Halliday's rifle. 'Adelaide. More wankers there than blowflies at a meat works. Every one of them with a French letter in his Bible for a bookmark.' He waved the rifle. 'Adelaide. If this were Big Bertha, I would blow the place to smithereens.'

'Take your dirty hands off my rifle,' said Halliday. 'You'd another like your ever loving rafiki, you *compañero*. Sitting duck and trapped dingo only. Betcha.'

'Get rooted,' said Sheean, replacing the rifle.

145

Halliday took a step forward. This guy wasn't as hard as he pretended to be boiled.

'Jello,' said Halliday, letting a wild hunch spring, 'Mr Jello and Mr Carborundum. You and your *rafiki*, your ever loving.'

Sheean looked from Webster to Parkes in bewilderment.

Halliday said, 'You know. The soft-hard-soft routine. Mr Carborundum grinds them down. Mr Jello catches their guts when they spill them.'

'Never thought I'd have to say this to anyone. You're more shickered than I am.'

'Don't give me your soft shit, Mr Jello. Tell me about Mr Carborundum. Him and McAskill.'

'Tim told you. And it was the first I'd heard of it. They had a bit of a blue.'

'Yeah, but what about Mr Carborundum?'

'Og? Everyone knows I only met him when he lobbed here to cut out his final cheque from Tim. Right, Des?'

Halliday did not hear Parkes confirm what Sheean had said. The pain had him and the pain had changed. The pain had wings and was lifting him, its claws biting deeper as it lifted him higher and higher.

New York lay below him, the roots of its skyscrapers growing from a humus of black plastic garbage bags. He fell from the pain towards that shining blackness.

Sheean had seen too many men in the light from death's door. He ducked under the bar flap only to collide with a shivering Sudan who had been helped up the stairs from the cold room by Vodka.

Parkes, rushing to go through the bar flap in the opposite direction, shouted, 'You blokes haven't been at the beer again?'

'Too cold for beer down there,' said Sudan, waving a bottle of rum.

'God's sake.' Parkes grabbed the bottle and went through to the

146

other side of the bar where Webster was slapping Halliday's face. Parkes gave Webster the bottle of rum. 'Try this.'

Webster took a swig from the bottle. Parkes said, 'I meant him.'

Webster took another swig. 'He's had more than enough.'

Halliday groaned and Webster slapped him again. Halliday rolled over, coughing. He pushed himself into a crouching position, a boxer taking a count, his eyes far away.

Parkes said to Webster, 'Think I should call the Flying Doctor for advice?'

Halliday reached for the bottle of rum. 'I know what I need and it's not a doctor's advice.'

44

Ogilvie snored, sprawled on his bed in the Bachelor Quarters, his feet bare and twitching where a lone ant scouted future possibilities.

The fridge hummed. Ogilvie dreamt that he was paraded, tallest on the right, in the full dress uniform of the Regiment.

In front, an altar of drums. Behind it, the colonel-in-chief as beautiful as she'd been the first time he saw her as one of the men in her first guard of honour.

The Regiment's colours, rich with battle honours, snapped in a wind which screamed out of a white sun, higher and higher and brain-scrambling.

The brain-scrambling scream half-woke Ogilvie into a memory of McAskill's lecturing. 'You men who were infantry of the line must realise that as members of the Special Independent Counter Insurgency Company, you will know no lines and no uniforms. In this new warfare, one might say warfare of the postnuclear future, your enemy is where you find him.

'If you do not find your enemy first, he will find you. And what

147

he will want from you is what you want from him: intelligence to enable main force commanders to take all appropriate measures for the restoration or maintenance of law and order.

'You are designated Special because you are now troopers with cavalrylike mobility, not privates.'

The fridge hummed on, lullabying Ogilvie back to sleep and to his dream in which all the rich curves of the battle honours on the Regiment's colours now changed into the face of his old mucker, Rodd, mad eyes staring his last, sane message, 'Get me home.'

'Shug,' Ogilvie shouted in his dream, 'I would've died to get you home only I didn't have your guts.'

In a hollow square about Rodd were rank upon rank of men, pig-snouted in gas masks. Behind their visors, the eye sockets of skeletons stared blankly.

And a sea that lapped their boots was blood in which other men in full fighting order swam.

'No,' shouted Ogilvie in his dream.

'Yes,' said the colonel-in-chief, bending a skeleton face to kiss him.

Ogilvie knew his dream was a dream. Yet he did not want to wake. The colonel-in-chief's lips were warm and right royal in their command. He put his arms around her.

There was no breath in him. Only hers. He wakened. Sue Cornwall's hair was flooding over him, trapping sunlight in a glow about her face.

She touched his eye where Donaldson had got in a punch. Ogilvie winced. She ran her hand down his right arm to the long, fading, reddish and blue mark. 'That bruise hurt, too?'

'Not a bruise.'

She kissed it. 'What?'

'What I am.'

His one certainty. She lay on the narrow bed beside him. He

turned to her. Her mouth was quick on his. Honey. From the swell of her breasts, she flowed to one place.

Home.

A swan beating down the mist and rising white from the dark loch near the Institute, its bugling answering the bugle of the morning on the barracks square.

A salmon leaping to find its birth waters.

He found her and she carried him on the wings of her thighs to another kind of certainty. Yet when he came home in her, she cried out as if the certainty were all his, holding the strength of it and him in her.

'My dear and only love,' he said.

She kissed him once more. 'Nice,' she whispered, 'Say it again.'

'Not me. A poem.'

'Say it,' she whispered, and he moved with her as she rolled him over.

'In the clover,' he said and laughed.

She laughed in reply, astride him now. 'Say it again,' she whispered, bending over him, her hair flooding red on his face. 'Say it.'

But he was already saying it in another way. She matched him, smiling, her eyes closed, her breasts in his hands as they journeyed and came together into each other's loneliness.

She lay alongside him. 'That's the first time,' she whispered.

He didn't say anything.

'The first time,' she whispered, 'I've laughed with a man in bed.'

He laughed, too, 'My, you're bonnie,' he said, 'I can't make up my mind whether it's the freckles or the creaminess of you. Rare.'

They kissed again.

Then, drugged with each other, they slept. Above them the coffin waited and in the doorway Ashby, who crept forward. His instant camera flashed as summer lightning to their closed eyes. When the instant camera had delivered its picture, Ashby could

149

not resist trying for a sequence of shots with another of his cameras.

By the doorway, her golden sandals. By the table, her shift dress, bronze gold with the wrinkled shimmer of silk, a skin she had cast to come to Ogilvie Eve-new. The long valley of her spine. The curve of her buttocks. The fullness of her breasts, breaking against Ogilvie's lean hardness. Her red hair lapping his shoulder.

Shooting his sequence, Ashby knew that the camera was an excuse for his detachment, not its reason. Tembo could be right. Camera big juju. It intensified detachment into a kind of pleasure. He moved closer to get a different angle on Ogilvie. The remembered click and purr of Ashby's camera opened Sue Cornwall's eyes. She twisted round in the bed and was for a shutter's click playing to the camera.

Ogilvie caught the play and Ashby. 'I'll swing for you, you toerag,' Ogilvie shouted.

She tried to hold him in the bed. Another mistake because Ashby knocked off another shot. Ogilvie said quietly, 'Is that it?'

Bollock naked, he rushed at Ashby, who retreated shooting and laughing. 'Can't say I blame you, Sue.'

She followed Ogilvie from the bed and tried to hold him again. 'Don't,' she cried. 'He's not worth hitting.'

Ogilvie halted. But not at her cry. He shook her off. Out of his confused anger had come the realisation of how McAskill had conned him.

'The so-and-so,' he said. 'The cunning, wee so-and-so. He knew what I would do. Every step.'

'Ashby's a creep's creep,' she said.

'Not him. McAskill. Colonel Kenneth McAskill, Special Independent Counter Insurgency Company. Him. That cold shite, McAskill.'

She tried to laugh. Another mistake. Ogilvie picked up her shift dress and threw it at her. 'Out,' he shouted. 'Out.'

Dustbin inched towards the dingo's carcase on her belly, whimpering. From the dingo's head and down his back ran a black stripe which rose buzzing when a crow swooped and braked on flapping wings to land on the dingo's back.

Snarling, Dustbin leapt. The crow rose and hovered, cawing among the buzzing flies.

Sniffing through the camp, Dustbin stopped to swallow one of the cooked mussels and crunch on an old beef bone. Below the scent of her dingo mate, she caught the fainter scent of Ogilvie. She trotted to the river and swam across, angling upstream as if to rid herself of the smell of death.

The wind was in her face when she came out of the river. A frill-neck lizard was almost in her shadow before it stretched its frill in defiance. A remnant instinct made Dustbin point, giving the lizard time to scuttle off on its hind legs. Dustbin followed a black streak led by a black shadow. The lizard dodged round a clump of salt bush and doubled back.

The scent of her pups came to Dustbin. She forgot the lizard and loped towards the clicking vanes of a windmill, beside which was the ruin of a pioneer homestead. One stone corner stood, a straight prow against the waves of sand. In the corner, protected on one side by the remains of a side-saddle and on the other by the remains of the works of Marie Stopes, were Dustbin's pups.

They yelped towards her, three of them now strong enough to be nipped into quietness. The fourth, the runt of the litter, was chewing feebly on a corner of the side-saddle. Dustbin began licking the runt.

46

Ashby sat at the table in his cabin, listening to Halliday's voice on the tape recorder.

'Trouble with you, Fisi, you don't understand. Appetite without comprehension is what you are. Rotten hyena in guts of literature but you don't know whether guts are genius or jerky.

'You don't understand. I'm a live ammo guy. That's what people read between lines in my books. Death's but-but-but. Live ammo. Dead flesh. Spearhead times. Europe, Asia, Africa. Yeah, and South America. Now you want Australia A to Zee.'

Ashby extended his hand. Halliday's voice rose. 'I'll give you Australia. Australia is continent stolen from original inhabitants who'd maintained its uniqueness from dawn of time by people who proceeded to turn it into imitation of everywhere from Pasadena to Manchester, from London to Naples, from Dublin to Athens and all suburbs in between.'

Ashby giggled as Halliday sang in a broken growl. 'Captain Cook came to Oz, sailing on a coal boat. Stuck a feather in his ass and called it Pax Britannica.'

The singing died. Ashby examined the instant picture he had taken of Sue Cornwall with Ogilvie. He picked up a book of matches lying on the table and struck one, preparing to burn the picture. Halliday's voice forced itself on his attention. Ashby blew out the match and put the picture in his shirt pocket.

Halliday was saying, 'These Australians are caught between awestruck and aw-fuck. Want two chickens in every pot and two chips on every shoulder. Can't seem to stand on their own two feet. Maybe weight of all those chips. First they had Auntie Britannia to hold their hand. Then Uncle Sam. Ever notice when they insult Uncle Sam they speak American. Next year, betcha, year after,

152

they'll have ayah from Indonesia.

'Yeah, sweet, little, bucktoothed Devi Poppins in sarong holding their hands instead of Uncle Sam and changing diapers instead of Auntie Britannia.' Halliday paused and Ashby heard him drink before continuing. 'Old bitch Britannia. Uncle Sam needed her. But where was she? Holding on to first and last colony, Ireland, that's where, old bitch, drawing lines where she fancied, as in Africa. Drawing line to mark off Northern Ireland from Ulster and then suggesting both the same. Old bitch Britannia accusing Uncle Sam of imperialism in 'Nam.' Halliday had another drink and a belch. 'Get this, Fisi, and get it good. What Jews were to Germany, Irish are to England – glory of its culture and its greatest shame ...'

The cabin door crashed open. Halliday stooped to come through the doorway, firing his rifle from the hip at the tape recorder.

Halliday's voice died in a whirr and a whine. '... old bitch Bri ...'

Ashby stayed in his chair as Halliday ripped the tape cassette from the recorder. He smashed the cassette and pulled a tangle of tape from it which he thrust into Ashby's mouth. 'You're going to have my guts for memoirs, Fisi. May as well get some chewing practice in.'

Ashby chewed on the tape for a moment and spat it out. 'Impossible to swallow.'

'Nothing's impossible for hyenas to swallow. I've seen a hyena eat its own guts and die fulfilled.'

'What about an elephant,' said Ashby, 'who recycles his own droppings for public consumption?'

Halliday reached Ashby in two roars, picked him up by an arm and leg and threw him, whirling, across the cabin onto the bed.

'Time you got yourself laid,' said Halliday.

Ashby snapped the photograph of Sue Cornwall down on the bedside table. 'I should try your lady. She's the ace of hearts around here.'

153

Halliday studied the photograph. 'Wrong ace.' He pointed at Ogilivie. 'Ace of spades.'

He turned for the door, reloading his rifle. One of McAskill's aces. Had to be. Old street reporter Halliday could still put one and one together to make a deadline.

47

Boondoo was making a chain from the ring can pulls which Bel's kids were fossicking for up and down the track and in and out of the old humpies.

When the chain was long enough, he held it out, shining, to Bel. She nodded. Boondoo split the chain. One half he handed to Bel. She watched him, and the kids watched too, as he joined the ends of his half together. He put the chain over Bel's head and round her neck so that it hung between her breasts.

'One wife woman, Bel,' he said, 'you.'

Bel joined the ends of her half together. Boondoo bent his head. Harold, laughing, snatched the jockey cap off so that Bel could get the chain round Boondoo's neck.

'One husband man, Boondoo,' she said, 'you.'

All the kids were laughing. Bel gave them boiled fruit cake and told them to have a drink at the tap. She made a fresh billycan of tea for Boondoo.

'Plurry lovely,' he said.

'Lovely if you stick to tea. No more all that grog.' She handed him a slice of cake. 'Eat.'

'Promise.' As he ate, he looked round the raft of concrete and at the tin shacks, thatched with brushwood. 'Fixing this place up real beaut.'

'Our place,' she said. 'Going to put shade all over here.' In the

154

air, she sketched the square formed by the tin shacks. 'Hole for fire. Cook out here. Smell of cooking inside house.' She pulled a disgusted face. 'Balanda sheilas, they don't care. All watered with flower stuff from those scent bottles and stinking allersame roo stew.'

Boondoo, laughing, went to the shacks. 'Og, he fix.'

'Bit,' said Bel. 'He help. I help. Kids help.'

'That Og. He tell me once, place he been. All houses, all roofs same these houses. White abos belong that place.'

'White abos. Og been shickered. And you maybe.'

'Og, he say white abos. Their country all about taken away allersame our country.'

'What name belong that country?'

'Ireland.'

'Ireland. Ireland. Father belong my father come from that country. He white abo for sure.' Bel took the billycan from Boondoo and drank. 'They still there, those white abos?'

Boondoo nodded. 'Think so, yeah. Og, he reckon they mighty men.'

Bel passed the billycan back. 'That country still their country, those white abos. Allersame this country still our country all around.'

Boondoo thought about that. 'Maybe. Maybe more better you and the kids come along Bobbie and me.'

Suddenly Bel reached and grabbed the jockey cap from Harold's head. She gave it to Boondoo. 'Other kids need their school time. Bobbie horseman. Same as you. Pretty to watch.' She cuffed Harold who was howling for the jocky cap. Harold dodged away. Boondoo caught him and put the jockey cap on him again.

'Harold,' said Boondoo, 'and Bobbie. Lubra and Myall. Two jockeys. Two horses. One father man Boondoo. Me.' He went back to the fire. 'Next day, tomorrow. Hooroo.'

155

'Long walk that way,' said Bel.

'Good country.' Boondoo drew a line with his finger in the dust on the concrete raft. Along the line he drew circles. 'Plenty water all along down there.'

'Them jockey men have coloured shirts.'

Boondoo took the big scarf from round his neck. He unfolded it to show Bel the yellow roundel on a red and black background. 'This colour our shirt.' He went over to where Bobbie was rubbing Lubra down. He held out the last piece of cake. Bobbie patted his lean stomach. Boondoo broke the cake into fragments and gave them to the other kids.

Bel waited by the fire. Boondoo unbuckled the belt that was under his shirt. He brought it across to her. She saw that it was made from a double strip of blanket.

'Proper kuri woman, you,' said Boondoo. 'Never mention this.' From the belt, he took one of the wads of dollars with which it was lined and gave it to her.

All this time Boondoo's daughter Olga had sat quiet as a shadow, waiting with the didjeridu. Now Boondoo, sitting down beside her, took the instrument. Resting the end of it on the earth, he blew his life into the mouthpiece. The kids became Olga quiet, their lives linked through Boondoo's life to the lives that stretched back to when the first breath was put into man.

Bel rocked slightly. Another child sought her breast. She knew them, everyone. Gary. Boondoo played on, moving the music forward to the high road and the low road his balanda mate, Og, sang about. Boondoo knew he was not making the music. The music was making him. Lifting him out of himself so that he could see all the camps down to Melbourne and hear the roar of the crowd as Bobbie brought Myall to the front in the final stretch.

156

48

Halliday shucked off his sweat-blackened safari jacket. The sun struck down, lasering into his bare back. The pain moved sideways. Burn, you son of a bitch, burn. Halliday picked up his rifle and peered through its telescopic sight at the beer can one hundred yards to his front.

'Coat of arms of Australia,' he shouted, reading his windage in the movement of the heat shimmer, 'beer can rampant on a female supporter with crosshairs.'

He fired. The beer can flew twinkling from the shelf on the old dressmaker's dummy and landed rattling on the track.

Off to the right, Bel's kids, Eddie and Shane, appointed target masters by Halliday, clapped their hands, faint echoes of other shots, other times.

McAskill in 'Nam. Observer under journalist cover, penetrated by old street reporter Halliday after McAskill had talked war. 'You Americans invented mass production. And that includes the mass production of death. Thus your boys waste, using their weapons like garden hoses. My - our men aim and kill.' One call to a contact and not only McAskill's slip was showing. His background, too. And his special unit. But he was unfazed when confronted with the information. Knew a thing or two himself, McAskill. Knew about Halliday's Irregulars. And how to mix a negrita of flattery, salted with condescension. 'I see Halliday's Irregulars as progenitor of the kind of independent formation you have so cleverly discovered I command. What a pity *you* did not get a chance to engage the enemy in Africa.' Knew why French still had face in 'Nam. Their stand at Dien Bien Phu. So understood concept of the Alamo option. How it offered the chance to hold the Saigon embassy, as the Texans held the Alamo way back in 1836.

Saigon embassy could've been held. For price of a lousy helicopter Navy tipped over the side. McAskill knew that, too. Naughty McAskill. Serving officer, holding Her Majesty's Commission, offering to act as broker for mercenaries. 'There are still those ready to hold the sum of things together for money, Mr Halliday. I can put you in touch.'

Pain and the wild hunch leapt together. Mad, black marlin with a hook in it. Fisi'd set him up for McAskill, and McAskill's goons were here to waste him because he knew too much. Three cheers for McAskill and his goons, Mr Carborundum and Mr Jello, for the hard-soft team.

Halliday sighted on the old dressmaker's dummy and it was McAskill in the crosshairs dealing with the objection that the Alamo option had to be American. 'All special formations share an elite awareness. Mr Halliday. They're the Praetorians of the future who recognise each other's quality. Recruiting Americans for you should present no problem if your price is right. I myself once recruited a Russian, or more exactly a Georgian Spetznat, Soviet special forces, for a little exercise involving penetration of the Kremlin. A training exercise, you understand.'

Halliday shouted, 'I understand, you prim son of a bitch,' and fired. The old dressmaker's dummy teetered on the cart: McAskill worried about what old street reporter Halliday's gen would do to his upward mobility.

Halliday fired again and the old dressmaker's dummy was knocked over into the dust: himself, dying in the besieged ruins of the Saigon embassy.

'With Alamo patriots,' Halliday shouted, 'like William B. Travis, Jim Bowie and Davy Crockett. Not mercenaries.'

He waved to Eddie and Shane. They set the dressmaker's dummy upright again and put a beer can on its shelf.

'Dollar a yard,' Halliday shouted. 'Lay anyone a hundred he can't hit a beer can at a hundred.'

He turned towards the pub verandah where Webster and Parkes, Sudan and Vodka, Boondoo and Sheean and Ashby and Donaldson leant against walls and posts, amused shadows in the shade. Two by two, Halliday noted and said, 'Touch of Walt Whitman and the trolley-car conductor about these Australians, Fisi – or have you been too busy enjoying it to notice?'

Ashby lifted his big watch on his wrist. 'Time you had something to eat, Tembo.'

Halliday took a can of beer from the garbage bag at his feet. 'I am something to eat, Fisi. You know that and you've served me up.' He waved Eddie and Shane to move the dummy closer. 'Fifty yards. And I'll still pay one hundred to anyone who hits beer can before me.'

Boondoo cracked his stock whip. 'Bang bang allersame Hopalong Cassidy,' he shouted. Donaldson laughed. Sheean gazed at the garbage bag of beer and ice. And at the bundle of dollars, weighted with a stone, next to it.

He stepped from the shade of the verandah. 'Can't think without a beer,' he said.

'Help yourself.' Halliday grinned. To get Mr Carborundum, he first had to get Mr Jello but he hadn't expected to get Mr Jello so quickly.

'Tell you what I'll do,' said Halliday. 'Two to one. Hundred of yours gets two hundred of mine if you hit beer can at fifty.'

'I'll think about it while I'm having this.' Sheean opened the beer and returned to the shade of the verandah.

Boondoo laughed and cracked his whip again. Halliday's rifle came up. The round splintered a piece from the verandah post above Boondoo's head.

Sudan touched the spot. 'Think you've got white ants, Des,' he said. 'Place can't last another year.'

They all laughed. Halliday glared at Boondoo and levered another round into the breech. 'Bloody *nugu*. Stop laughing or I'll string you up with your own whip.'

Ashby smiled. Classic case. Show the old fool a picture of his woman with another man and he goes into a courtship display with his rifle. Well, not so much rifle as a lever-action dildo whose sperm was death, to quote from Scott Halliday's *Under the Flame Tree*.

Halliday was shouting, 'Do I have to make it three to one at twenty yards?'

Donaldson straightened. 'I'll be in that for fifty.' He removed his hat and counted the money in it. 'Yeah, fifty. Three to one. Twenty-five yards.'

Halliday waved Eddie and Shane to pull the dressmaker's dummy into position. Then he handed Donaldson a can of beer.

'Later,' said Donaldson.

'Now. Rule of Tembo Halliday All American Beer Can Shooting Club. Drink one before you shoot one.'

Donaldson opened the can and drank, letting as much as possible run down his chin. Tim Webster brought him a rifle from the four-wheel drive.

'She loaded?' said Donaldson.

'Yeah, with peas,' said Webster.

Donaldson grunted, aimed and fired. The beer can went flying. Immediately, Halliday said, 'Double or quits. Double distance. Double bet.'

Donaldson shook his head. 'Enough for a good booze-up's enough for me.'

Halliday counted him out his winnings and Donaldson went back to the verandah where he handed the rifle to Tim Webster.

'Be in it,' said Donaldson.

Webster tugged at his nose. 'Taking enough off him as it is.'

The old dressmaker's dummy stood untouched. Halliday raised

160

his rifle. McAskill was in the crosshairs again. McAskill in London. 'Most disappointing the way your Saigon embassy fell, Mr Halliday. Most. I rather expected to see you and your New Model Irregulars on the television reraising Old Glory after the departure of your Marines. After all, the Alamo option was your idea and it did call for a Custer. Wherever were you?'

The old dressmaker's dummy teetered at Halliday's shot. 'Prim son of a bitch. The only history you know's your own and you won't learn from it. Custer had nothing to do with the Alamo. He was Little Big Horn. You know where I was when the embassy fell. Same place you were. But you weren't under cover of journalist there.'

He turned to Sheean. 'You know, too, Mr Jello. So what about a bet? Or are you into trapped dingos and sitting ducks same as your *rafiki*, your ever loving Mr Carborundum?'

Sheean whispered to Webster, 'Troppo. He's gone troppo. You better get him out of the sun before his brains turn to lamb's fry.'

'Already have,' said Webster. 'He won't come out of the sun till his money's gone.'

Sheean touched the rifle Webster held. 'That one hasn't got a telescopic sight. His has. Unfair.'

'Aw, look, I don't know about that,' said Webster. 'Weren't you in the Army?'

Sheean nodded.

'Open sights there. Unless you were sniper.'

Sheean held up his swollen right hand. 'Don't know how I'd go with this.'

Des Parkes said, 'I'll do the other one. That'll even you up.'

Sudan said, 'Lend us a few dollars and we'll show him what a rifleman can do.'

Sheean took out the roll of dollars and counted it for the first time. 'Five hundred and seventy-five.

161

'I can cover that,' said Halliday. 'Bet is you can't hit one at two hundred.'

'Make it the even five hundred,' said Sheean, handing the extra seventy-five dollars to Sudan.

Halliday gave him a can of beer and Tim Webster the rifle which he had reloaded. Sheean drank the beer slowly. Something about Tembo Halliday's All American Beer Can Shooting Club was puzzling him.

When he sighted on the dummy, Sheean realised that one of the things that was wrong with Tembo Halliday's All American Beer Can Shooting Club was himself. He was drunk. Two dummies and two cans swayed slowly in front of him. He closed one eye and lined up the sights. One dummy. One can. Was it the right one? He fired on the question. His bullet hit the empty beer can. And he got the answer to the other thing that was wrong with Tembo Halliday's All American Beer Can Shooting Club.

'You fixed the rules in your favour,' he shouted at Halliday.

'Don't get excited, Mr Jello. You've won. How's about double or quits?'

'No chance. You make sure the other bloke drinks first and shoots first.'

Sheean was stuffing his bet and his winnings into the pockets of his blue overalls. Sudan O'Brien came from the verandah and took the rifle from him, saying to Halliday, 'Fifty all right on one at two hundred?'

'Sure.'

'You shoot first.'

'Sure.'

'And drink first.'

Halliday grinned as the pain reached round from his back. Go ahead, you son of a bitch. Go ahead. I'll waste you before you waste me.

Aloud he said to Ashby, 'You've got the pocketbook, Fisi. Let's have some more of Uncle Sam's sovereign specific against the ills that flesh is heir to.'

Ashby laid a bundle of dollars at Halliday's feet. 'Five thousand.'

Sheean stared at the money. Most he'd seen since the $35,619 which had been strictly a steal. Could he ever win enough to pay the steal back? Not this side of Hell.

Halliday finished drinking a can of beer. He threw the empty can away from him in a high arc. His rifle came up. He fired, sending the can jinking in the air. While it was still falling, Halliday pivoted and got off a second shot which sent the can on the dummy flying.

'Sorry, mate,' said Sudan, 'but we're not dead yet.'

'Don't worry,' said Sheean, heading for the Bachelor Quarters. Main thing was to put Og's money back in his boot before he discovered it was gone. Then Og might not follow him when he shot through on the plane.

Through the telescopic sight of his rifle, Halliday watched him. Could take Mr Jello out now. But Mr Jello had money fever and would be back with Mr Carborundum.

Sudan said, 'What odds will you give us about three at three hundred? We've still got twenty-five here.'

Halliday looked into Sudan's eyes, red-rimmed from years of sand and glaring distance. 'Ten to one. Three cans at three hundred yards.'

Sudan took the three full beer cans Halliday passed to him and shouted to Vodka, 'All right, you reffo bastard. We've got a bet. Let's see what we can do.'

Boondoo's stock whip cracked and cracked again as Vodka came from the verandah to drink the cans of beer opened for him by his mate, Sudan.

49

The wind brought Dustbin the smell of the remains of the kid she and her dingo mate had brought down in the morning. She resensed the surging excitement of the hunt, the panic of the goats and the blood taste. She knew exactly where they had hidden the remains of the kid in the shade of two rock slabs leaning against each other.

She nipped and nuzzled her litter behind the old side-saddle. When she had them all safe, she licked the runt and moved on the line for the remains of the kid.

All the litter stayed behind the side-saddle except the runt who followed her, yelping. Dustbin turned in her track below the crest of a red sand hill. The runt was trying to struggle up the slipping side of the sand hill. Dustbin went down, picked the runt up by the scruff of its neck and carried it back to the remains of the homestead. She nuzzled the runt back behind the old side-saddle where the other pups began to nip it.

Dustbin let the runt suckle again and the others so that they slept. She herself slept before moving out again from the homestead.

The smell of the kid meat was stronger now and the wind lifted from the crests of the sand hills a fine spray of red sand which caught the sinking sun.

As Dustbin traversed the red sand hill again, she heard rifle fire. Danger. But also fresh meat and a black shadow in which she had walked. A voice she had followed. 'Here, girl.' She halted below the crest of the sand hill.

When a cock crowed from the chook run, Dustbin turned and, keeping below the skyline as her dingo mate had taught her, trotted towards Rainbow.

50

Ogilvie had a white canvas tarpaulin spread out on the floor of the Bachelor Quarters and was laying his gear on it ready for rolling into a swag.

Sheean said, 'You're mad. Blind stabbing off to nowhere.' He looked towards the door as two shots sounded from the track. 'There's money to be had out there.'

'I've got enough,' said Ogilvie, 'and I'm not blind stabbing. I know where I'm going.'

And he did. Back. Because now he knew why McAskill had turned up at Tim Webster's camp: to inspect the prisoner, 621 Trooper Ogilvie, A.

Simple Og who hadn't realised at the time the easy way he'd escaped meant they wanted him to escape. Bringing him for court martial by ship not by plane. And via Glasgow. The way the provost escorts took the handcuffs off and suggested a drink in the pub before the train south.

They knew a prisoner and a provost escort in a pub, any pub, in Glasgow would be bound to cause a rammy. They knew his training would take him straight back to the docks to find the first ship sailing. McAskill's training.

They hadn't wanted him to appear before the court martial. Not on a charge involving Her Majesty's Government's methods in Ireland. Not with the newspapers already kicking up a stink about torture.

Ogilvie pulled on his blue shirt and tucked it into his shorts.

Sheean said, 'The plane tomorrow. Wait.'

'I've waited too long.'

Ogilvie laid his shaving gear on the tarpaulin. All he'd done was escape to jail – the biggest jail in the world with the blue sky for a roof, the sun for bars and mirages for walls. McAskill had only come to have a dekko at him, doubling under his load of guilt, up and down the years, chased by the ghost of his mucker Rodd.

Three more shots sounded. Ogilvie went outside to the water tap and screwed a length of hose to it. He turned the tap on.

'Wait for the plane,' said Sheean.

'I marched in.' Ogilvie played the hot water on himself. 'I'll march out.'

'You're round the bend, ready for an asylum.'

'Been in one.' Ogilvie turned off the tap. There was no cleaning himself that way. He stared at Sheean, baggy, blue overalls black in the dimness of the Bachelor Quarters. 'I've got to tell you,' Ogilvie said. His head bumped against the water bag hanging in the doorway as he hurried back inside. Down his forehead a drop of water ran. A good memory. The strongest. Stilwell the padre had done his best work with water. Only one way to get clean again. 'I've got to tell you,' Ogilvie repeated.

He fell on his knees in front of Sheean and was silent, trying to clear his mind now that the moment had come. The asylum. If. If only he'd been able to march out of the asylum with his mucker Rodd. Get him home, get his mucker Rodd home from the asylum where they had hidden him after he went off his head under torture. That would've been something. Getting his mucker Rodd home would have been something. And he should've been able to with the asylum unguarded.

Not like the top-security, white-noise room his mucker Rodd was interrogated in, went mad in. If only. Big bloody if.

Getting into the asylum had been a doddle. Hadn't he once trained to penetrate the Kremlin? But inside the asylum. Bad. Bad. His mucker Rodd dying in a jacket that buttoned up the back, staring his last, sane message, 'Get me home.'

Easier to lift mad and quiet, his mucker Rodd, than sane and

166

fighting. But the other poor loonies, bawling the odds, wanting to come too. That had put the kibosh on things.

Should've formed up the loonies and marched them out to take over the city. Aye, that would've been the shot. All the loonies in their nightshirts taking over from the lads in their gas masks and flak jackets and the boys with their begged, borrowed or stolen guns and their home-baked bombs.

His mucker Rodd would've done that. Hadn't his brag, 'Easy! Easy!', carried their whole intake through basic training? Wasn't he the only recruit in the Regiment ever to call Sergeant Alisdair De Ath 'Sergeant Death' to his face? 'Easy! Easy! Sergeant Death!'

Ogilvie made the sign of the cross. Sheean laughed. 'Bloody Presbo comedian, you've been on the grog again,' he said and began scattering money from his pockets over Ogilvie.

'I baptise you,' Sheean shouted, 'in the name of the dollar and of the cent and of the holy interest, amen.'

'God's sake,' said Ogilvie, 'what're you doing?'

'Giving you back your money,' said Sheean.

Ogilvie picked up a twenty. 'Mine?'

'Well, ours. I invested yours.'

'You –' Ogilvie reached for his boots and felt in the toes – 'You stole it. You stole my money.'

'Invested it.' Sheean gathered the money together. 'We share it.'

'Keep it. If you needed to steal it, you need it more than me.'

'We both need it.' Sheean split the money. 'More than enough here to get us on the plane tomorrow.' He held out a wad of notes. 'Your original five hundred and seventy-five plus hundred and twenty-five interest.'

'Bugger interest,' said Ogilvie, 'just give me what's mine.'

'Just,' said Sheean, 'just.' He counted $125 off the wad and held the rest out to Ogilvie.

Ogilvie took the money and stood up. Faster he went back, less chance he would have to change his mind about telling. Fly all the way. Straight back. No messing.

'Where'd all this other money come from?' he said. 'Pinch it as well?'

Four shots sounded. 'Game of skill,' said Sheean. 'The big Yank reckons he can outshoot, outdrink anyone. He's playing drink a can, shoot a can – for real money.'

'That a fact?' Ogilvie sat down on his bed and pulled on clean socks.

'Sorry,' said Sheean.

'I'm the one who still has to say sorry,' Ogilvie said, lacing up his best boots. 'When I do, you'll be there.' He bound the puttees round his ankles.

'Here. I'm staying here.'

'You're coming with me. All the way. I need you.'

Ogilvie snapped on his belt and bayonet, picked up his rifle and two clips of ammunition and went into the sun. Sheean was stuffing money back into his overalls when Ogilvie returned, went to the fridge, took out the jug of goat's milk and finished it off in a couple of long swallows.

'Beauty,' said Sheean, following Ogilvie out. Time enough to give Og the slip in the morning. Get him on the plane, then hop off at the last minute and keep on hopping till he reached that commune. Meantime, he might get a few more dollars to feather his nest in the commune. And he would really be able to enjoy it, knowing old Og was flying back to Pommieland with enough to shout the bar.

51

Bel came from behind the dress rack in the storeroom, wearing the frock she had chosen earlier.

Mary Parkes said, 'So when is the wedding to be?'

'Wedding today,' said Bel. 'My man pay for frock.'

'But this morning you told me you didn't know who he was.'

'Know now. My man Boondoo. Him and me married.'

'But who married you?'

'He married me. I married him.'

'I mean who performed the ceremony? After all, my husband is the local justice of the peace.'

'Sunday is day of rest.'

'Witnesses,' said Mary Parkes.

'All the kids saw us. They tell you when you be teacher again. You tell your man. My man Boondoo going Down Below. He going Melbourne Cup way with his horses and my Bobbie and Harold.'

'You can't let him take your children away just like that.'

'He give me more,' said, smiling, and left Mary Parkes clutching the money she had paid her for the frock.

52

Halliday reloaded his rifle as Vodka returned to the verandah and Sudan's. 'Reffo bastard, I set it up for you. Four cans and we would've had enough for a real holiday.'

Vodka shrugged. Halliday said, 'You win some. You lose some.' His daddy had told him that when they used to match pennies. What would his daddy say if they had to match pains? Never give a cancer an even break?

Boondoo's stock whip cracked a welcome to Ogilvie and Sheean. Halliday shouted, 'You going to give me chance to get my money back, Mr Jello? Double and double. Double the distance. Double or quits. Drink can before you shoot can.'

'I'm shooting,' said Ogilvie. 'See us the beer.'

Halliday took four cans from the bag. 'We're on four at four hundred, Mr Carborundum. Don't have to ask whether you have any money.'

Ogilvie laid his wad on the ground. 'This says I can do it.' He began to drink off the beer.

Up on the verandah, Des Parkes said to Boondoo, 'Let's forget the deal. But what about a little side bet? Two thousand says the Yank beats your mate Og.'

'Og can shoot.'

'My money's on the Yank to win.'

'I haven't got your kind of money.'

'One of your horses then. Only one. Myall against two thousand.'

Boondoo considered while Ogilvie loaded his rifle and lay down in the prone position to fire.

'All by the book,' said Halliday, 'and Lee Enfield. Gun that lost the British Empire.'

'Don't try to chat me off my game, Yank.'

'I thought McAskill's boys were into the unorthodox, is all.'

'McAskill. What's he to you?'

'You know, Mr Carborundum.'

'I know you're full of wind.'

'Careful, Mr Carborundum. You won't find me as easy as my woman.'

Sheean smiled. So that's what was bugging the Yank. He was wearing the horns. And that's what was bugging Og. He'd been unfaithful to his colonel-in-chief, the princess.

'Interested in a side bet?' Sheean said to Halliday.

'Sure, Mr Jello.'

'Another two fifty.'

'Great.'

Ogilvie concentrated on the targets balanced on the dressmaker's dummy's shelf. He hooked his left arm through the rifle sling for extra steadiness and his cheek came against the butt. 'Kiltie, kiltie caul' bum. Cut his teeth on a rifle butt.'

'By the book,' said Halliday.

Ogilvie ignored him and adjusted his rear sight.

On the verandah, Des Parkes whispered to Boondoo, 'You on?'

Boondoo saw Bel coming in a long, white frock and said, 'Sorry, boss. My missus wants me to bet everything on us.'

'Make it three thousand against Myall,' Des Parkes whispered, 'and free grog, win or lose.'

'Off grog, boss. And got plenty money to buy what I need,' said Boondoo. 'Even potato chips.'

Des Parkes registered the mischief in Boondoo's eyes before they slid away from his. Bloody boong, what did he mean?

Ogilvie fired his first shot and hit a beer can.

'The receipt,' Des Parkes shouted, jumping from the verandah and going across to Ogilvie. 'The receipt for the horses. Boondoo's. You put it into the potato–chip packet and Boondoo ate it. You're no better than he is, bloody abo through and through, you mongrel bastard.'

Ogilvie did not move from his firing position. 'Easy on the hard words, Des. Or you'll find yourself eating them without any teeth.'

'Well, you did.' Des Parkes shuffled his false teeth into a scowl and Halliday noted how he was backing away not from Ogilvie's words but from his quietness.

'Not me,' said Ogilvie.

'It flaming well was.'

'Not really me, Des. It was my old mucker Rodd.'

171

'I don't know him from a bar of soap.'

'You would've liked him, Des. He's just remembed me of the fifty-two I owe you. Help yourself.'

Des Parkes took fifty-two notes from the pile near Ogilvie and went back to the verandah.

Ogilvie took aim again, his breath held. He'd said Rodd's name aloud and his three remaining shots and hits saluted it. A volley over a soldier's grave. The echoes of the shots, a summons to return and tell them on the Institute's barracks square what he had done.

Halliday watched Ogilvie retrieving the spent cases. Mr Carborundum was McAskill's man all right. Mr Carborundum was *simba*, a lion. Halliday put his sleeveless safari jacket back on and began to reload his rifle. The end could begin.

53

Mary Parkes whacked the plastic swatter down on the fly crawling towards the sugar bowl. Triumphantly, she held up the swatter. The fly was sticking to the mouth embroidered on the swatter with red raffia. Yellow raffia had been worked into pigtails on either side of the swatter and black raffia had been used for eyes.

'Clever,' said Sue Cornwall.

'Yes, it is clever, isn't it?' said Mary Parkes. 'Des always brings me a couple of dozen plain ones when he goes Down Below. I embroider them and send them down for the fete.'

'Worse than death?'

'Beg pardon?'

'What fete?'

'The girls' school. Sacred Heart. They love it. I knew they would. I loved it myself.'

Mary Parkes poured another cup of tea for her guest and passed her a slice of jubilee cake on a silver trowel. Sue Cornwall picked up the white napkin from beside her cake plate and tied it round her neck. Mary Parkes stared in surprise. Sue Cornwall was unaware. Yet the effect of the white napkin contrasted with the red of her hair and the bronze gold of her shirt dress caused Mary Parkes to touch her throat and then the apple-green belt she had tied round her hair.

'I like doing that, too,' she said.

Sue Cornwall was puzzled and took a bite of jubilee cake. Mary Parkes explained, 'Using things in different ways, the way you used the napkin.'

'I wasn't thinking,' said Sue Cornwall. 'It was something I used to do at home when I was little.' She moved to untie the napkin.

'Don't,' said Mary Parkes.

'I like your dress,' said Sue Cornwall. 'The colour and your eyes.'

'Yes,' said Mary Parkes, feeling free to go to the conversation she'd first thought of, 'the sisters were all delighted when I told them about Des.'

'How many sisters do you have?'

Mary Parkes laughed. 'Not my sisters. The nuns. I mean Des wasn't as rich as some of the matches they made novenas for but as Sister Marie used to say, "Wealth is not everything". Now your ...' She took a sip of tea and raised her white napkin from her lap. 'Your ...'

'Delicious jubilee cake,' Sue Cornwall said, taking another bite. 'Your ...'

'Tembo Halliday isn't my husband. And he's not my keeper.'

'My word, I'm sorry if. The fact is. Up here, a new face. I didn't mean to be a sticky-beak.'

From the track, five shots sounded. 'Men,' said Mary Parkes.

She smacked at another fly and missed. She moved to the kitchen

173

off the parlour. 'Funny the things you remember. Sister Marie always used to tell us how important white gloves were. Now the only ones I ever wear are these.' She pulled on a pair of green rubber gloves.

The transceiver crackled the call sign Delta Hotel Lima Seven. Mary Parkes waved her rubber-gloved hands. 'Get that for me, there's a dear.'

Sue Cornwall spoke into the microphone. 'This is the pub at Rainbow. Over.'

'Good day, Mary. Mae Morrison here. Can you tell me whether that Sue Cornwall you have staying with you is any relation of Vicky Cornwall? Over.'

Sue Cornwall smiled. 'Yes, daughter. Over.'

'Imagine that. Victoria Cornwall's daughter with a man old enough to be her father. Makes you think. Over.'

'What does it make you think? Over.'

'You sound a bit funny, Mary. As if you'd swallowed something. She's not there listening by any chance? Over.'

'Yes, I am. Over.'

'Oh, dear. Over and out.'

Mary Parkes was bent over the kitchen sink trying to stifle her giggles with a green rubber glove. 'Terrible gossip, old Mae. Take the whole Snowy Mountains hydroelectric scheme to keep her in power for chatting. She must've been listening in when I mentioned your name earlier.'

'But my mother,' said Sue Cornwall.

'Where did she go to school?'

'Girton,' said Sue Cornwall, 'in Adelaide.'

'I know where Girton is,' said Mary Parkes. 'And so does old Mae. And does she skite about it. Girton, Girton, Girton. The way she talks you would think it was the only school in the world.'

'Well, I've heard people say it's quite good.'

Six shots rang out. Mary Parkes rattled the dishes. 'Is Tembo Halliday often like that?'

'I don't know. He *is* old enough to be my father but I've only been travelling with him for a little while.'

'Gee, it must be exciting. All those different places with someone like that.'

Ash from Sue Cornwall's cigarette fell on the floor as she nodded. Mary Parkes produced a mop from a cupboard and wiped the floor clean. 'I would have loved to travel. I mean, I have been to Sydney but everyone there seemed to have been somewhere I hadn't been.'

She moved to the table to pick up the dishes. Typical. This girl wasn't much help in a chat and less with the dishes. She rattled the dishes in the sink. Sue Cornwall said, 'Anything I can do to help?'

'Get the gun.' Mary Parkes was staring out of the kitchen window.

'What?'

'The shotgun. Next to the sideboard. Get it.'

Sue Cornwall brought the shotgun. 'Undo the fly screen.' Mary Parkes giggled. 'And stand by to pick me up.'

The sound of the fly screen being undone alerted Dustbin near the chook run. She was turning and running as Mary Parkes jabbed the fly screen open with the gun barrel, brought the gun to her shoulder and fired. Dustbin checked, blood blossomed on her rump. She ran on.

Mary Parkes sat down giggling. She looked across at Sue Cornwall, who was shaking. At first, Mary Parkes thought she was giggling too and her own giggling redoubled. Then she realised Sue Cornwall was sobbing.

'Was it the blood?' Mary Parkes said. Sue Cornwall kept sobbing. 'Do you want Mr Halliday?' Mary Parkes said.

Sue Cornwall wanted Ogilvie. To travel with him. She could not stop sobbing. 'What an idiot I am,' Mary Parkes said. 'It's that

175

time of the month, isn't it?' Sue Cornwall shook her head, still sobbing. Not that time of the month. That time of life when the past catches up with the present and shows the way the future is going to be. The past. The Starway Modelling Academy and Nelly Carpenter and her certainty. 'Sell yourself, Suzie sweetie. Sell yourself – otherwise you might as well be a wire coat hanger in an empty wardrobe.'

Mary Parkes offered a glass of brandy. Sue Cornwall shook her head. She had sold herself. And her child. For sure. For money. Which was why she knew she would not be able to persuade Ogilvie the pictures weren't prearranged with Ashby.

'You'll be all right in a minute,' said Mary Parkes, sipping the brandy herself. 'Blood does that to some people.'

Blood. Sue Cornwall stood up. But there had been no blood with Ogilvie. And that was another regret. She went to the kitchen sink, washed her face and dried it with the white napkin which she then retied about her neck.

Mary Parkes said, 'Must tell Des' and unhooked a speaking tube from behind the window curtain.

54

Des Parkes was in the bar giving himself a rum when the speaking tube whistled. He picked it up, listened and ran outside.

Halliday's shadow was long on the track. His rifle came up, black against the bright, blue sky. He fired and hit six times. And fired again. And missed.

Sheean roared with delight, raising a can of beer. Parkes fronted him. 'Ought to shove it down your throat.'

Sheean lowered the can. 'Sun getting to you?'

'The sun's not getting to me. I'm flaming mad, you bloody

bludger.' Having worked himself into a big enough rage, he turned on Ogilvie. 'That bitch of yours has been after my chooks.'

'Sorry to hear that, Des.' Ogilvie had a pile of dollars at his feet. He held a handful out to Parkes. 'What's the damage?'

'She didn't get anything. Mary shot her.'

'Dead?'

'Wounded.'

'Maybe Mary ought to shoot against the Yank here.'

Halliday's rifle swung on Ogilvie. 'I've got your number. You're one of McAskill's specials.'

Ogilvie held Halliday's fierce stare. The old Yank had somehow made the right connection but he was getting the wrong message.

'Yeah,' Halliday went on, 'not B-Special. Specialists' Special.'

'It's a shirt full of ribs you're asking for,' said Ogilvie.

'No,' said Halliday, 'I'm not.' And thought, got enough pain for rest of my life. Pain crazy. Fox crazy. 'Double or quits on everything you've got, I kill that bitch you're son of before you do.'

Ogilvie looked at the pile of notes between his feet. 'You're on.' He released the magazine from his rifle and Halliday watched the steady deftness with which he reloaded and snapped the magazine back. A *simba* OK.

'The stakes,' said Sheean, 'I'll hold them.'

'No way, Mr Jello,' said Halliday, 'Tim does.'

Ogilvie nodded. Webster began to gather the money together. Sheean tried to help. Des Parkes pushed him aside and helped Webster who looked at the sun and took his watch from the lee of his paunch.

'Get set,' he said, and watched the second hand sweep round to twelve. Should he tell them they didn't have much shooting light left? He glanced at Ogilvie, then at Halliday. No-hoper versus

177

bullshit artist. The second hand hit twelve. 'Go,' said Webster, 'And may the best bastard win.'

Ogilvie doubled away. Halliday followed. Before they had gone five steps, Boondoo was ahead of them, circling to cut Dustbin's blood trail. He gave a cooee when he found it and Ogilvie led Halliday in pursuit.

The blood trail ended at the river. Bondoo waded across first. Ogilvie and Halliday followed, holding their rifles chest-high. Olga imitated them with the didjeridu. Bel and the other kids crossed lower down where rocks provided stepping stones.

Mary Parkes and Sue Cornwall waited while Ashby and Don- aldson and Vodka and Sudan crossed behind Bel and her kids.

Tim Webster and Des Parkes brought up the rear, counting the stake money as they went.

'You stay here,' Des Parkes said to his wife as he waded into the shallows. Mary Parkes waited until he was across and followed on Bel's stepping stones.

Sue Cornwall hesitated. Mary Parkes called from midway across, 'Come on.' Still Sue Cornwall hesitated, her gaze moving from Ogilvie to Halliday and back again. 'Come on,' Mary Parkes called from the other side of the river. 'Can't let the blokes have all the fun.'

Sue Cornwall crossed on the stepping stones. As she did, she took the white napkin from her neck, soaked it in the river and retied it.

Mary Parkes had gone on ahead. Sue Cornwall hurried to catch her, not much liking the sense of being enveloped by the bird-noisy bush.

Halliday stepped from the shadow of a termite tower. She attempted to avoid him. He got in front of her. 'I'm too old for tag,' he said, 'and I think you are, too.'

'I don't want to talk to you.'

'*Mimi ni nyama, wewe kisu.* You're still the knife, Bibi, and I'm still the meat. But maybe I know what you want better than you do.' He reached out his hand and began loading his rifle from the bullets on her black belt. 'And maybe those honeybees will get you what you want.'

'In that case.' She unbuckled the belt.

He caught it as it fell from her waist. 'Later,' he said, and did his mock-stuttering bit. 'F-f-f-aking eagerness no good now.'

'Creep,' she said.

He rebuckled the belt, slung it across his chest bandolier style and jogged off, saying, 'Okay, Bibi. I'm the creep. But you're still the knife.'

She waited until he was well ahead of her before following his track.

55

Boondoo ranged ahead into a gully. He found what he was looking for in a dry gum leaf turned across the drift of others and further in a pebble less sun-bleached than its neighbours.

Halliday watched Boondoo working, hand holding a twig as if he were divining the spoor.

The gully debouched onto a dry, grassy paddock. Halliday knelt, scrabbled a handful of dust and threw it into the air. Wind from north. Few thorn trees instead of gums – lion country. He stood up. Oglivie was keeping ahead of him. Lion country and *simba*.

Boondoo, bent almost double, got a whiff of the dingo, fading now. Mixed with it was Dustbin's smell. She was following up an old track of the dingo's which dropped off the dry grassland down a steep slope.

On the edge of the slope, Boondoo waved Halliday and Ogilvie to him and began to explain what he thought Dustbin was doing. The chatter of the kids interrupted him.

'More like picnic race,' he said. 'All you kids stop your yabber.'

The kids became silent, passing on the threat in his voice to each other in shoves and scuffles.

Boondoo said, 'Reckon that dog not bad hit. No more blood.' He waved his twig, taking in the slope, the broken country at its foot and the waves of red sand beyond. 'Down along there.'

Des Parkes said, 'Tim and me are judges. First man to kill Dustbin takes the pot.'

'Yeah,' said Sheean. 'You're a real judge all right. It's double or quits.'

'Shut up,' said Des Parkes.

Tim Webster held out a thick wad of notes. 'Four thousand six hundred. And it's double or quits.' He spoke directly to Halliday. 'You can cover that?'

'No problem. Might have to be traveller's cheques though.'

Webster turned to Ogilvie. 'That OK with you?'

'Definitely,' said Ogilvie, 'I'm travelling.'

'I can change traveller's cheques,' said Des Parkes. 'Only a small additional charge.'

'You would sting your grandmother and then ask for her bum,' said Sheean.

Halliday grinned to cover a spasm of agony. Ultimate sting. Sting of death. But he had the cure. He glanced at Ogilvie. A simba, McAskill's goon'd turned into a simba. The way he'd said, 'I'm travelling.' Cool. *Simba* concealing imment charge under lazy front, soft growl.

'When you're ready,' said Webster.

Ogilvie surveyed the ground ahead all the termite towers. 'Keep the kids well back, Boondoo, will you?'

'Water bottle,' Halliday said. Ashby gave it to him. Halliday

180

took a swig and spat in disgust. 'Shit and derision, Fisi. When I want one of your Madison Avenue Martinis, I'll ask for it.' He threw the water bottle at Ashby.

Ogilvie moved then, doubling down the slope, his rifle held high and clear of the scrub. Halliday stood rigid. The pain had changed again. No longer the sharp clasp of a creature swimming. Nor of a bird. The pain was female. A witch whose nails were red and deep in his guts and stopping him following his cure.

Ashby's motor drive purred and clicked. Halliday glared into the camera lens and took one slow step and then another.

Ogilvie was halfway down the slope. He stopped and looked back. Halliday raised his rifle above his head. The shrapnel and gold ring on his finger gleamed.

'Son of a bitch,' he roared, setting off down the slope after Ogilvie, 'Son of a bitch,' his roar echoing in his mind. Son of a bitch, you're going to do me a favour and you don't know it.

So headlong was his rush that he almost fell, and was afraid again. Broken neck no good. Witch pain needed bullet. Not silver bullet. Aimed round.

Ogilvie was now moving forward cautiously. Halliday passing him at a run, gave him a jab with his rifle butt. 'Move, son of a bitch.' Ogilvie stumbled. Even as he went sideways with the stumble, he was bringing his rifle to bear on Halliday's back. Sudden as a memory, one of Bel's kids was in the line of fire. Ogilvie lowered his rifle. There'd always been kids getting in the sights when he'd done sniper duty. These people fought with their kids. So did the abos against those who wanted them tidied out of sight.

'To me,' Ogilvie yelled, 'to me.'

The kid ran to him while the setting sun pressed a last breath of wind from the day. Ogilvie held the kid – himself, himself watching from behind the five brass buttons with the coat of arms of the Montrose Military Institute for Boys on them as the townies went

181

walking with their mothers and fathers. 'Kiltie, kiltie caul' bum. Nothing but a wee orphan. Kiltie, kiltie caul' bum. His maw was a craw and his paw ran awa'.'

Bel lifted the kid into her arms. 'Gary, I been told you. Stick with me.'

'Aye, do that, son,' said Ogilvie.

Halliday had swung south to keep the wind on his cheek. 'Son of a bitch,' he roared, 'get the lead out.'

Ogilvie went after him, leaping over rocks and dodging among the termite towers. As he passed Halliday in his turn, Ogilvie shoulder-charged him. Halliday reeled against a termite tower. Part of it crumbled off and Halliday, leaning against the tower, watched its tiny makers move blindly to repair the damage. He picked a pinch of dust and termites between his finger and thumb and put them in his mouth and swallowed them. 'Repair me,' he whispered, bowing his head. 'Repair me.'

When Halliday looked up again, Ogilvie was two hundred yards ahead and holding to the west. Halliday moved after him, grinning. Mr Carborundum should come out of the setting sun. And would, when brought to bay.

Halliday cleared his throat and spat. Women were wrong. Men could get pregnant. With their own death. God's last laugh.

56

Ashby fitted a long lens onto his motorised camera and focused on Halliday leaning against the termite tower.

'Old fool,' said Ashby, clicking off a shot. 'He hasn't got the legs to be playing partisans and Krauts any more.'

'He can shoot,' said Donaldson, 'that's for sure. Hope to hell he takes every bloody cent that big Pommie bastard has.'

'Beat up on you, didn't he?' Ashby switched to his instant camera and focused on Donaldson's face. 'Poor boy.'

Donaldson scowled into the instant camera. He didn't want this poofdah Yank's sympathy or his pictures. Time to choke him off. 'You're so far up yourself, I don't know how you get down for a crap, let alone to take pictures.'

Ashby was left holding the newly developed photograph as Donaldson drifted towards Sue Cornwall. She wanted it. Donaldson knew she did. Ashby dropped the photograph and darted round to get a long-lens shot of Halliday leaning against the termite tower. This time framed between Donaldson and Sue Cornwall.

When Halliday moved off after Ogilvie, Ashby swung the camera with Halliday and began clicking off shots: Halliday leaping over a rock, rounding a termite tower, halting to survey the terrain ahead.

Ashby swung the camera away from Halliday in search of the dog. Tembo with his rifle loaded needed a kill or he wouldn't settle down for a taping session.

57

Dustbin was moving her pups from the ruined homestead when Ogilvie saw her. She carried the runt by the scruff of its neck in her mouth. The three other pups followed her.

'Here,' Ogilvie called. 'Here, girl.'

But Dustbin ignored him and she was his ticket back to where he needed to be. He lay down in the prone position, took aim, fixed Dustbin in his sights, aimed off a fraction. 'Kiltie, kiltie caul' bum, cut his teeth on a rifle butt.' He could not squeeze off the round. Not at Dustbin who was his past, his only boyhood, and Bran, the Institute's mascot.

One hundred yards behind, Halliday stopped. Mr Carborundum

was still doing things by the book. Have to get him out of that and into his gut instincts. Halliday raised his rifle. Dustbin was silhouetted in the crosshairs. Halliday traversed till he found the last pup in the line. He grinned. Pity they weren't flying. He killed them from the rear. One, two, three. His fourth shot blew the runt from Dustbin's mouth in bloody fragments. His fifth shot cut Dustbin off in mid-howl.

His sixth shot zipped over Ogilvie's head. Ogilvie rolled over into dead ground and twisted round to face the direction of the sixth shot as Halliday roared, 'The bitch you're son of is dead. Pay up, loser.'

Halliday peered into his telescopic sight, trying to find a sign of movement. There was none. But he spotted Ogilvie's Balmoral where it had caught in a bush when he rolled into cover. He held on the Balmoral, roaring, 'Loser because you're a coward. One of McAskill's Specials. He told me how he picked them. Infantry of the Line, he told me. Turn them, he told me, and they'll do anything.'

'And you did, Mr Carborundum. You practised on blacks in Africa what you did to white niggers in Ireland.'

Ogilvie risked a shufti. Halliday was in full view, the rifle barrel growing from his white head like a black horn. What was it Vin had said? 'Old enough to be your father.' Needed a fright, the old so-and-so. Aye, and a real fright, his father, scarpering, leaving his mother . . .

'And me,' Ogilvie yelled, 'Me. Me, you old –'

'Yeah, you, Mr Carborundum. You're part of the thin yellow line. Thin yellow line going back through Algeria to Frogs who collaborated with the Gestapo.'

Ogilvie waited. Sue Cornwall moved away from Donaldson and crept nearer to Halliday, who roared again, 'You gag them, Mr Carborundum, while McAskill blowtorched them? You fixed terminals on their balls? You the white noise expert turning up the volume to blow their minds?'

In the blindness of his own pain, Halliday remembered telling Sue Cornwall about her mind not being able to stand the pain in his mind and knew McAskill's secret: his mind could stand the pain he inflicted. He played God, substantiating what he already knew: all men break to display the truth that is in them.

McAskill. Prim son of a bitch'd known where old street reporter Halliday was when Saigon fell. McAskill was in some goddamn place. At wrong war in Nannie Britannia's first and last colony. Ireland. In Belfast yet, its grey face tarted up with lollipop colours, red, white and blue, green, white and gold. And only one thing agreed: white not for surrendering.

'White for torture,' Halliday shouted. 'White noise. Right, Mr Carborundum?'

Ogilvie did not move, did not reply. The old-so-and-so was in for the biggest fright of his life. And he would scarper.

Halliday held on the Balmoral. Be perfect if it were Praetorian purple and McAskill's head were in it. Way he'd played the tease about the Alamo option. Reason old street reporter Halliday was in Belfast was to check out turning public building into strong point in a city where hostiles would turn on you as fiercely as each other. Like family caught in incest. Violence as incest.

'The Alamo option was go,' Halliday shouted. 'Men, money, weapons. But no time.' He fired at the Balmoral. His bullet clipped the pom-pom from it. He grinned. White House painted white after British burnt it in 1812. Should've been repainted yellow after Saigon bug-out. Yeah, yellow with pinko stripes.

Ogilvie reached for his Balmoral. Halliday fired his pain. It seared across Ogilvie's hand. He pulled the Balmoral onto his head. As the echo of the shot died, Halliday heard a sliding rattle and snap. McAskill's man was fixing bayonet. Mr Carborundum was a *simba*, a lion with what witch pain needed, a steel claw.

'Son of a bitch,' Halliday roared, 'son of a bitch. I was ready for the Alamo option and I'm ready for you.'

Halliday knew he was over the top. Like drunk picking a fight. Understatement not his style. Leave that to English who needed it. Yeah, like lime juice. As specific against their scurvy hypocrisy.

'Son of a bitch,' he roared again, 'come and get what I've got for you.'

Ogilvie rose up, roaring in his turn as the sun licked along the rifle to the fixed bayonet and into Halliday's telescopic sight. Ogilvie charged out of the setting sun, charged, roaring, 'Easy! Easy! Sergeant Death!'

Halliday drew what he hoped was his last breath and held it, his rifle unwavering on the point of aim.

Sue Cornwall cried, 'Don't,' and pulled Halliday's rifle downwards as he squeezed off his shot. Ogilvie fell backwards as if he'd hit a wall and bounced off it, his roar was cut to 'Eas–', his arms jerked up, his rifle flew from his hands and landed in a patch of scrub.

Ashby laughed. 'Shot,' he said, lowering his camera. Sue Cornwall screamed. Halliday slapped her into silence. 'Crazy bitch. I was aiming over. Over. Way over his head to bring him on. On. To me.'

She was already running to Ogilvie who was flat on his back.

'You're joking,' she said, putting her hand under him.

'Aye, that's right,' he said. 'But I'm not so sure your old Yank was.'

She looked at her hand, expecting – hoping for sweat and saw his blood. She began to scream again.

Tim Webster ran to Halliday and took his rifle. Halliday kept repeating in counterpoint to the screams, 'I was aiming over. Over. Way over his head. To bring him on. On. To me.'

Mary Parkes held Sue Cornwall, stroking her red hair, soothing her screams to sobs.

Bel's kids came crashing through the bush, all legs and giggles. They halted and became silent at sight of Ogilvie. Bel, still carrying Gary, went to him.

Ogilvie swam up through his pain and, seeing Bel and the child, remembered Rodd's wife with her child, remembered her curse. 'God damn you to hell for a khaki Judas whose heart's as black as his boots.'

Ogilvie went down, down under his pain which froze over in despair.

Bel said, 'Oh, Jesus, Jesus, Og been close up finish. Oh, Jesus.'

Ogilvie heard the word and swam up through his pain again to break the icy despair. Bel, all in white, cloaked in the dusky blue of the sky, Bel and the child were now an image of sufficient grace.

'Vin,' said Ogilvie, 'get Vin.'

Sheean turned to run. But Vodka held him and said, 'You can't leave your mate.'

'He needs a doctor, not me,' Sheean said as Vodka pulled him towards Ogilvie. 'The Flying Doctor. I was going to get on the transceiver to the Flying Doctor.'

'Might be an idea at that,' said Sudan.

Sheean broke free and ran. Vodka went after him. 'Let him get on the transceiver,' said Sudan. But Vodka caught Sheean. 'You can't leave your mate,' he said. 'Is Australian rule.' Ogilvie rose to his feet, groaning, and staggered over to Sheean who broke free again. Ogilvie managed to get his arms over Sheean's shoulders and hooked round Sheean's neck. Sheean felt the weight of death on his back as he stumbled forward with Ogilvie whispering in his ear, 'Bless me, Padre.'

Sheean halted, trying to break Ogilvie's grip. 'Mad, Presbo comedian. You can't. Not me.' He stumbled on, dragging Ogilvie who whispered, 'I delivered a man to the specialists, the torturers – my mucker Rodd. He was never one for provost duty, my mucker Rodd. He joined the fighters in Ireland. And I delivered him to the specialists, the torturers who sent him mad. Aye, into the asylum. Ah, Christ, I couldn't get him out. He would've got me out, my mucker Rodd. Best man I ever knew in my whole life and I delivered him to the specialists, the torturers.'

'No,' Sheean said, 'not me. I've given it away.'

'You can't give it away. Stilwell told me,' Ogilvie whispered, and 'Oh, my God, I am very sorry that . . .'

Sheean tried to break into a trot to shake Ogilvie off his shoulders. 'Stilwell?'

'The padre who baptised me a Catholic. Like my mucker, Rodd,' whispered Ogilvie surprised that Sheean should've asked about Stilwell, so vivid was Ogilvie's memory of Stilwell going up in the afternoon to jump with the first refusers to reassure them.

So vivid now the memory of Stilwell growling Mass. Not like the chanting and smells and candles of the midnight Mass with his old mucker, Rodd. Stilwell growling fast. Like he was expecting mortar rounds instead of bells. Growling fast and then his voice slowing and sharpening to a command: *Hoc est enim corpus meum.* This is my body.

Ogilvie felt himself free-falling into blackness. His grip on Sheean relaxed and Sheean pulled free. Ogilvie fell face down on the ground and Sheean, turning, saw that Ogilvie's back had been blown open where Halliday's round had exited.

Sheean could not resist the wound. He could not bear it. He went back to Ogilvie and rolled him over so that the wound was hidden. Ogilvie jerked out of his freefall and opened his eyes. Sheean said, 'You'll be okay. The doc'll fix you up and you'll be home on the plane before you know it.'

'Cut the kidding,' Ogilvie whispered. 'I'm for the low road with Sergeant Death.'

He gripped Sheean's right hand. Sheean gasped at the pain in his hand, swollen from the mallet blow. Ogilvie raised Sheean's hand over himself. 'Say it, Padre.'

'I can't,' said Sheean, 'I'm a thief.'

'You'll do me,' Ogilvie whispered.

'Put it to the touch, Padre,' Ogilvie whispered. 'To win or lose it all.' And he began to move Sheean's hand in the sign of the cross.

As he felt the strength of Ogilvie's faith flow into his hand, Sheean realised Des Parkes had been right: Og was bloody abo through and through. But not in the way of the flagon as Tim Webster said – in the way Og believed the simplest rituals could carry the mightiest mysteries and crack eternity.

Sheean's right hand moved in pain with Ogilvie's dying hand and he heard himself saying the words he had never expected to say again, '*Ego te absolvo a peccatis tuis. In nomine Patris, et Filii et Spiritus Sancti.*'

Bel, holding Gary and with other kids clinging to her skirts, drew in a breath at what she recognised as Vin's monkey yabber.

Des and Mary Parkes exchanged a look of understanding. I absolve you from your sins in the name of the Father and of the Son and of the Holy Ghost.

Ogilvie also understood. 'Amen,' he whispered. His eyes closed. Sue Cornwall came and knelt across from Sheean. He put out his hand and took her tears on his thumb to anoint Ogilvie's eyes, ears and lips.

'*Proficere, anima Christiana, de hoc mundo …*' Sheean began and could not continue. Again Des and Mary Parkes looked at one another. Go forth, Christian soul, from this world …

Boondoo put his didjeridu to his mouth and began to play as he had played for Bel's kids, mixing the long past with the high road of life and the low road of death.

Ashby kept clicking off shots. 'Goddamn Fisi,' said Halliday. 'Give me my rifle and I'll put a bullet in his camera eye.'

Tim Webster swung the rifle by the barrel against a termite tower, once, twice, and handed it to Halliday. 'My bloody oath,' Webster said. And let the story start in his mind for the pubs and the years. Smashed Tembo Halliday's flash rifle. Yeah, the same one he used to shoot the sheep. Should've smashed it then. And maybe Ogilvie, you remember that big, mad Scotsman, would be alive . . .

Halliday threw the broken rifle into the bush. Sparrows, every-one counted, rose from a fence. Barbs take wings to sing, Halliday thought. And give that man another cigar.

Away, away, in the farthest reach of his life, Ogilvie heard the drone of Boondoo's music as a pibroch.

He struck through the sea of pain to win to the soldiers of the Regiment he could see standing at attention with their rifles to take the salute of the sharks on the troopship's sinking deck, while the Regiment's colour was trooped through their ranks. The escort to the colour was Colour Sergeant Sammy Abercrombie and Colour Sergeant Alisdair De Ath, bayonets fixed, rifles at the slope. The Regiment's colour, rich with battle honours, none richer, was carried not by an ensign but by Private Shugg Rodd who dipped it in salute to the colonel-in-chief.

'My dear and only love,' Ogilvie whispered.

Sue Cornwall caught the whisper for herself. She took the white napkin from around her neck and wiped the cold sweat from Ogilvie's face. She *was* the knife, as Halliday said. But a knife that felt pain. And the man on the ground was not meat. He was . . . She dared not define the hope she had. She could kill it as she had killed before.

190

Ogilvie swam on. His swim was seen by Sue Cornwall and the other watchers as a sprawling agony in which his arms flailed, his right hand opening and closing on the air as if to grab handfuls of it for his gasping lungs.

'Give him air,' said Sheean.

Vodka Mahonsky understood Ogilvie's agony. He fetched Ogilvie's rifle from the scrub where it had fallen and gave it to Sudan O'Brien.

'You rifleman,' said Vodka.

'I know that, you mug reffo. But there's no way I'm making a dying man's rifle mine.'

'Not yours,' said Vodka, 'his.'

. Sudan understood then, too. He went to Ogilvie and placed the rifle along his right side, setting its stock in the cleft between Ogilvie's thumb and fingers.

Ogilvie became still. His breath rattled, echoing the final command of his eyes. Sheean passed his right hand down over Ogilvie's eyes to close them, having received and understood their final command: the coffin to be carried by six bearers, slow marching.

Sheean glanced at Boondoo who continued to make his music. Boondoo, for sure. And Vodka, Sudan, Des Parkes, Tim Webster. Sheean glanced at Donaldson. What about this bloke? What if he didn't want to be a coffin bearer?

Sheean raised his fist. Bel said, 'Allersame Tarzan and more monkey yabber.' But Sheean only beat his chest with his fist three times and shouted, 'I'm Og's padre. Like Stilwell. What I say goes.'

Halliday lit a cigar. '*Simba amekufa.*' Was that a title? he wondered. *Simba amekufa.* The Lion is Dead.

Ashby crouched by Ogilvie to get a close-up of his face and switched to his instant camera. A flash flared, blinding in the setting sun, and the instant camera developed the colour photograph.

191

Ashby handed it to Halliday. 'The lion *is* dead, Tembo. Have this for your trophy collection.'

Halliday studied the photograph. Was this the story to go with the title? Great. Great the way the simba roared, 'Easy! Easy! Sergeant Death!'

Not so easy now. Halliday fingered his gold ring set with the mortar fragment. Death in close-up, cure for death wish. He watched as Sue Cornwall was helped to her feet by Mary Parkes. There would have to be an inquiry. Not his fault. Any case, Bibi would blame herself. And would need consoling. He bit into his cigar and grinned to hide another spasm of pain. Be still, witch. Or for you it's a brew of croc gall. Big African juju for curing pain with death. But not yet. Maybe he should let his pregnancy go to term. He studied the instant photograph again.

In the pallor of death, the truth of the long, bruiselike mark on Ogilvie's arm had been revealed by the instant camera as the red and blue tattoo of a crucifix. Instead of a halo, the Christ figure had a star of David behind its head. Halliday had seen such a tattoo before. He knew that its bearer had once been a pilgrim under arms in Jerusalem.

Halliday looked down at Ogilvie. He was no longer sprawled in agony.

The body of Ogilvie, A., Private, 621, returned to the Regiment, lay at attention, his best boots, scuffed by his charge, still had something of their parade shine, his rifle with fixed bayonet was by his side.

His spirit doubled towards that light to which all must come.